MOLLY FOX'S BIRTHDAY

Deirdre Madden is from Toomebridge, Co. Antrim. Her novels include *The Birds of the Innocent Wood*, *Nothing is Black*, *One by One in the Darkness*, which was short-listed for the Orange Prize, and *Authenticity*. She teaches at Trinity College Dublin and is a member of the Irish arts academy Aosdána.

DEIRDRE MADDEN

Molly Fox's Birthday

ff

faber and faber

First published in 2008
by Faber and Faber Limited
Bloomsbury House, 74–77 Great Russell Street,
London WC1B 3DA
This paperback edition first published in 2009

Typeset by Faber and Faber Limited
Printed in England by CPI Bookmarque, Croydon

A CIP record for this book
is available from the British Library

ISBN 978-0-571-23966-5

4 6 8 10 9 7 5 3

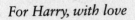
For Harry, with love

In the dream I was walking through the streets of a strange city, in a foreign country I did not recognise. I was weary, and my feet were sore because I was wearing shoes that were too small for me. Then, as is the way in dreams, I was all at once in a shoe shop and my grandmother was there. She did not speak, neither in greeting nor to explain what she was doing there, but handed me a pair of shoes made of brown leather. I put them on and they fitted perfectly. Never in my whole life had I had such soft and comfortable shoes. 'How much do they cost, Granny?' I asked. She told me the price in a currency I had never heard of before, but of which I somehow knew the value: I knew that the price she named was derisory, that the shoes were in essence a gift. And then she gave me a thick green woollen blanket and I wrapped myself in it, and it was only now, when I was warm, that I realised how cold I had been, and it was only now that I remembered that my grandmother was dead, had been dead for over twenty years. Far from being afraid I was overjoyed to see her again. 'Oh Granny,' I said, 'I thought we had lost you for ever.' She smiled and shook her head. 'Here I am.'

I awoke and I couldn't remember the dream. I only knew that I had been dreaming and that it had left me full of joy. Then immediately I was disconcerted by not recognising the room in which I had awoken. Whose lamp was this, with its parchment shade? Whose low bed, whose saffron-coloured quilt? The high windows were hung with muslin curtains, the room was flooded with morning light, and all at once it came to me: I was in Molly Fox's house.

Molly Fox is an actor, and is generally regarded as one of the finest of her generation. (She insists upon 'actor': *If I wrote poems would you call me a poetess?*) One of the finest but not, perhaps, one of the best known. She has done a certain amount of television work over the years and has made a number of films, a significant number given how much she dislikes that particular medium and that the camera, she says, does not love her. Certainly she does not have on screen the beauty and magnetism that marks out a true film star, and she hates, she has told me, the whole process of making a film. The tedium of hanging around waiting to act bores her, and the fact that you can repeat a scene time and time again until you get it right seems to her like cheating. She likes the fear, the danger even, of the stage, and it is for the theatre that she has done her best work. Although she often appears in contemporary drama her main interest is in the classical repertoire, and her greatest love is Shakespeare.

People seldom recognise her in the street. She is a woman of average height, 'quite nondescript' she herself claims, although I believe this fails to do her justice. Fine-boned, with brown eyes and dark brown hair, she has an olive complexion; she tans easily in the summer. She often wears black. Neutral tones suit her – oatmeal, stone – and natural materials; she wears a lot of linen and knitted cotton. On the dressing table of the room in which I was sleeping was a marquetry box full of silver and turquoise jewellery, silver and amber, together with glass beads and wooden bracelets. For special occasions she wears silks and velvets in deep, rich colours, purple or burgundy, which I think suit her even better than more subtle tones, but which she thinks too showy for everyday wear. She dislikes the colour green and will have nothing to do with it, for like many theatre people, Molly is extremely superstitious, and if she speaks of 'the Scottish Play' it is not only out of respect for the feelings of others.

When the public fails to recognise her in her daily life it is not just because they see her face only infrequently on the cinema or television screen. It is because she has a knack of not allowing herself to be recognised when she doesn't want to be. I have no idea how she does this, I find it difficult even to describe. It is a kind of geisha containment, a shutteredness, a withdrawal and negation. It is as if she is capable of sensing when people are on the point of knowing who she is and she sends them a subliminal denial. *I know what you're thinking but you're wrong. It isn't me. I'm somebody else. Don't even bother to ask.* And they almost never do. What gives her away every time is her voice. So often have I seen her most banal utterances, requests for drinks or directions, have a remarkable effect on people.

'A woman with such a voice is born perhaps once in a hundred years,' one critic remarked. 'If heaven really exists,' wrote another 'as a place of sublime perfection, then surely everyone in it speaks like Molly Fox.'

Her voice is clear and sweet. At times it is infused with a slight ache, a breaking quality that makes it uniquely beautiful. It is capable of power and depth, it has a timbre that can express grief or desire like no other voice I have ever heard. It has, moreover, what I can only

3

describe as both a visual and a sensuous quality, an ability to summon up the image of the thing that the word stands for. When Molly says *snow* you feel a soft cold, you can see it freshly fallen over woods and fields, you can see the winter light. When she says *ice* you feel a different kind of cold, biting and sharp, and what you see is glassy, opaque. No other actor with whom I have ever worked has such a remarkable understanding of language.

Unsurprisingly, she is much in demand for this gift alone, for voice-overs, radio work and audio-books. Although constantly solicited for it, she always refuses to do advertising. People who have never entered a theatre in their lives recognise her distinctive speech from historical or wildlife documentaries on television or from the tapes of classic children's literature they play to their sons and daughters in the car.

Now she was in New York and from there she would go to London to make a recording of *Adam Bede*. I thought of her sitting alone in the studio with her headphones and a glass of water, the hair-trigger needles of the instruments making shivering arcs, as if they too thrilled to the sound of her voice. I thought of the bewitching way she would call up a whole imagined world so that the sound engineers behind the glass wall and anyone who would ever hear her recording would see Hetty in the creamery as though they were there with her. They might almost smell the cream and touch the earthenware, the wooden vessels, as though Molly were not an actor but a medium who could summon up not those who were dead, but those who had never been anything but imagined.

She lives in Dublin, in a redbrick Victorian house, the middle house in a terrace. The front path that leads from the heavy iron gate to the blue-painted front door is made of black and red tiles, and is original to the house, as are many other details inside. There is a pretty, if rather small, garden at the front that Molly keeps in a pleasing tangle of bright flowers all summer, like a cottage garden. She grows sprawling pink roses, and lupins; there are nasturtiums, loud in orange and red, there are spiky yellow dahlias and a honeysuckle trained up a trellis beside the front window. Bees bumble and drone, reeling from one blossom to another like small fat drunks. Inside, the house is surprisingly bright and airy. There is a fanlight above the front door, which is echoed in the semicircular top of the window, high above the return, which brightens the stairwell. On the ceiling in the hall there is a plasterwork frieze of acanthus leaves, and a central rose from which hangs an elegant glass lamp. Although it has immense charm it is a small house, more modest than people might expect given Molly's considerable success. She bought it at the start of her career and has remained there ever since, for the sake of the garden, she says, although I suspect that Fergus is the real reason why she has never left Dublin. She also has a tiny apartment in London where she is obliged to spend much of her time for professional reasons. She likes the city; its vast anonymity suits her temperament. My home is also there, and I am always pleased when she says she is going to work in London, because it means I will have her company for a few months. She is without doubt my closest woman friend. This particular visit, to make the Eliot recording, coincided with her getting some urgent work done on her London flat, and I was interested in spending a little time in Dublin, so I suggested that we simply borrow each other's homes, an idea that delighted her, for it solved her problem at a stroke.

I heard the clock in the hall strike the hour and counted the beats. Six o'clock: still far too early to get up. I lay in Molly's wide soft bed knowing that in less than a week she would be lying in mine, and I wondered what it was to be Molly Fox. Slippery questions such as this greatly preoccupy both of us, given that I write plays and she acts in them, and over the years we have often talked to each other about how one creates or becomes a character quite unlike oneself.

In spite of my own passion for the theatre, unlike many other dramatists there is nothing in me of the actor, nothing at all. When I was young I did appear in a couple of minor roles in student productions, which served their purpose in that I believe they taught me something of stagecraft that I would never have known otherwise. But I have never felt less at ease than standing sweating night after night under a bank of hot lights, wearing a dusty dress made from an old curtain, pretending to be Second Gentlewoman and trying not to sneeze. 'You must stop immediately,' one of my friends said to me. 'I know you want to write plays but if you keep on with the acting, you'll lose whatever understanding you have for the theatre. As an actor, the whole thing becomes false to you. I know you believe the theatre has to be a complete engagement with reality or it's nothing. If you guard that understanding and bring it to bear on your writing, you'll be a terrific playwright, but if you keep on trying to act, you'll undermine your whole belief in the theatre. And as well as that,' he added, with more truth than tact, 'you're easily the worst actor who ever stepped on a stage.'

I have considerable experience of working with actors over the years, and yet their work remains a mystery to me; I believe that I still don't know how they do it. Molly will have none of this, says I have an innate understanding of what they do, and that it's just that I don't know how to explain it. She says this isn't a problem, that most actors can't put it into words either, and that many who do speak confidently about it aren't to be trusted. She also says that there are as many ways to be an actor as there are actors. Once I said to her that I thought what she did was psychologically dangerous. I sometimes think she is more in danger of losing touch with herself than I am, that something in her art forces her to go deeper into herself than my art requires of me, and that the danger is that she might lose her way, lose her self. 'But it isn't me!' she exclaimed. That contradicted something she had said to me once before – that if she, Molly Fox, wasn't deeply in the performance then it would be a failure.

Eventually we decided, after much discussion, that our different approaches to character could be seen as a continuum. For me, as a playwright, the creation of a character is like listening to something faint and distant. It's like trying to remember someone one knew slightly, in passing, a very long time ago, but to remember them so that one knows them better than one knows oneself. It's like trying to know a family member who died before one was born, from looking at photographs and objects belonging to them; also from hearing the things, often contradictory, that people say about them, the anecdotes told. From this, you try to work out how they might speak and how they might react to any given circumstance, how they would interact with other characters whom one has come to know by the same slow and delicate process. And out of all this comes a play, where, as in life, people don't always say what they mean or mean what they say, where they act against their own best interests and sometimes fail to understand those around them. In this way, a line of dialogue should carry an immense resonance, conveying far more than just meaning.

For me, the play is the final destination. For Molly, it is the point of departure. She takes the text, mine or anyone's, and works backwards to discover from what her character says who this person is, so that she can become them. Some of the questions she asks herself – *What does this person think of first thing in the morning? What is her greatest fear?* – are the kind of questions that I too ask in the course of writing, as a kind of litmus test to see if I know the character as well as I think I do. She begins from the general and moves to the particular. How does such a person walk, speak, hold a wine glass? What sort of clothes does she wear, what kind of home does she live in? I understand all of this, and still the art of acting remains a mystery to me. I still don't know how on earth Molly does what she does and I could never do it myself.

What kind of woman has a saffron quilt on her bed? Wears a white linen dressing gown? Keeps beside her bed a stack of gardening books? Stores all her clothes in a shabby antique wardrobe, with a mirror built into its door? Who is she when she is in this room, alone and unobserved, and in what way does that differ from the person she is when she is in a restaurant with friends or in rehearsal or engaging with members of the public? Who, in short, is Molly Fox?

I was reluctant to pursue this line of thought because I suddenly realised that, lying in my bed in London next week, she might do exactly the same thing to me. Given her particular gift she would be able to reconstruct me, to know me much better than I might wish myself to be known, especially by such a close friend. But no such reservation had touched Molly when she was showing me around her house a few days earlier to settle me in. 'Make yourself completely at home. Take whatever you want or need and use it. If there's something you can't find, look for it.' She hauled open a drawer and stirred up its contents to show just how free I should make with her things. 'This is good, wear this,' and she took the linen dressing gown from its hook behind the door, tossed it on the bed. When I protested mildly against this unlimited generosity, she replied in a voice not her own, 'Oh come now, my dear, don't be so middle class,' a voice itself so larded with pretension that I could only laugh. What she offered me was far more than I wanted or needed. I thanked her for her kindness and told her to treat my own place in exactly the same way, even while I silently hoped that she wouldn't. And yes, I did feel guilty because it was a mean-spirited thought.

I knew how fond she was of her home and everything in it, something that was difficult to square with her attitude of non-attachment. Take our mutual friend Andrew, for example. I'm even closer to him than to Molly, and I've known him for longer too, but he would never give me the free run of his home, of that I'm certain. Not that I would need it anyway, for he also lives in London, and I wouldn't want it because of the responsibility. While Molly's house is full of stylish bric-a-brac, unusual but inexpensive things that she has picked up on her travels, pretty well everything Andrew owns – vases, rugs, furniture – is immensely valuable. Worrying that I might spill a glass of red wine over some rare carpet or mark an antique table with a cup of coffee would take away any pleasure in staying there. Given how clumsy I am it's always a relief, even when visiting him, to leave without having broken or damaged anything.

Andrew. He had been much on my mind of late. I had hoped to see him before I left London. I had called and left a message on his answering machine, asking him to ring, but he hadn't got back to me. No doubt this was a particularly busy time for him. His new series had started on television the previous week; the second part would be shown tonight. I had wanted to wish him the best for it.

Yawning, I stretched out and switched on a small radio on the bedside table. The music that came from it was hesitant and haunting, a piano played with a kind of rising courage, the notes sparse and scattered with a yearning quality that somehow seemed to match the mood of the morning: it was, at least, what I needed to hear. What would I do today? I would spend the morning working in the spare bedroom that I had set up as an office for the time that I would be here. Because it was Saturday I would give myself the afternoon off and go into town. I knew that I had had a pleasant dream just before I awoke but I couldn't remember what it had been about. I looked again at my watch and decided it was still too early to get up even though the room was flooded with light. It was the twenty-first of June, the longest day of the year. It was Molly Fox's birthday.

I saw Molly on stage before ever I met her. When I was in my last year at university, at Trinity in Dublin where I read English, I went one night to see a production of *The Importance of Being Earnest*, hoping that I wouldn't be disappointed. All my life I have used this play to discover what people really know about the theatre, as opposed to what they think they know. Anyone who dismisses it as a slight, rather empty piece of entertainment immediately falls in my estimation. Too often it is staged in a stale and complacent way which suggests that the director also holds it in limited regard. But this production, by a young company called Bread and Circus, wasn't at all like that. While fully exploiting the elegance and wit of the language, it also brought out the darker side of the play, the snobbery and the social hypocrisy, Wilde's yearning to be a part of something that he knew did not merit respect. *Never speak disrespectfully of Society, Algernon. Only people who can't get into it do that.* Didn't he know that he was worth the whole lot of them put together, and that by not assuming superiority he was only bringing himself down to their level and setting himself up for his own destruction? By the use of Irish accents for certain characters this production subtly addressed a colonial aspect of the play that I had never thought about until then; and it also brought out the sexual politics of the work, the pragmatism and deception. They were a young company, and while that was a part of their strength, giving them their wonderful irreverence, their willingness to take risks, it was also part of their weakness. None of them was over thirty, a distinct disadvantage for playing Miss Prism or Lady Bracknell; and some of the acting was frankly poor.

But the young woman playing Cecily was outstanding. So fully and naturally did she inhabit the part that it was impossible to see how she was doing what she was doing, to deconstruct her art into its component parts. Her remarkable presence and charisma were not dependent on her looks, for she was not particularly pretty, and her only distinguishing physical feature, waist-length dark brown hair, I took to be a wig. But there was the voice of course, that beautiful, musical voice. During the interval when the lights came up in the shabby theatre, I took out my programme to see who she was, and I noticed several people around me do the same thing. In the course of the following months I saw her in other plays and noticed her name in the papers. Even when a production was comprehensively panned, she always seemed to escape censure. *Only the singularly gifted Molly Fox emerges with honour from this sorry hotchpotch of bad direction and shoddy acting.*

Around the time I left college – I think it was just after Andrew had left for England – something uncanny happened to me one day. I was at a table in a café when I noticed a young woman sitting nearby, with a cup of coffee and a book. Her face was familiar and yet I couldn't place her. Perhaps she was also a student at Trinity and I knew her face from seeing her in the library or passing her in the squares, without ever having spoken to her. She was wearing a black leather jacket and draped over her left shoulder was a dark brown plait, shiny, and stout as a rope that might tie up a ship. With that, I realised who she was: so it wasn't a wig after all. She picked up a small brown packet of sugar and shook it hard so that the contents fell to the bottom, tore it open and poured it onto the froth of the coffee. For the next half-hour she read her book and sipped at the mug, while I watched her. Nothing else happened. I have described it as an uncanny incident, and it was. I did not approach Molly – what could I possibly have said? *I really liked you in 'The Importance of Being Earnest'*. And what could she have replied? *Why thank you very much*. What would that have amounted to? Less than nothing. There are forms of communication that drive people apart, that do nothing other than confirm distance. But there are also instances when no connection seems to be made and yet something profound takes place, and this was just such a moment.

I realised the enormity of her gift. I had been aware of it when watching her on stage, but seeing her here in the café, unrecognised, anonymous, confirmed it for me. It was hers in the same way that her thick pigtail was hers, complete, real, undeniable, hers to do with as she thought fit. I believe that this was clearer to me then than it could have been to Molly, for how we see ourselves, our future, is often tainted by the very hope of what we wish to become. I was at that time already a person of enormous ambition. I knew even then that nothing except being a playwright could ever reconcile me to life; but my gift, I thought, was only a spark. I had none of the effortless brilliance of this other woman. As was the case with Wilde himself, we are at each moment of our lives the persons we were and shall become. The convict in his arrowed uniform who wept on the station platform as people screamed abuse and spat at him had been present years earlier when the same man had been hailed triumphant on the first night of his theatrical success. In the same way, the actor who would give some of the most profound and intelligent performances that one could ever wish to see on stage was already there in that young woman with her coffee and book.

I like to think that she looks exactly the same as she did when I knew her first, but it isn't true. The Molly of today is far more groomed and poised than the person I saw in the café all those years ago. The long hair, the leather jacket, the casual slick of lipstick have all gone, but they went gradually, so that her transformation, as is the case with most people, happened slowly over time. It is only now, by making a conscious mental effort or by looking at old photographs, that I can recall her as she was, and I can pinpoint no one day, or even a particular time in her life, when she suddenly appeared to me as having completely changed.

And what had I been doing in the café on that day? By a strange coincidence, jotting down notes for the play I had just begun to write, and which would make both Molly's reputation and mine the following year. It was based upon my experiences in London the previous summer, when I had worked as a chambermaid in the morning and as a domestic cleaner in the afternoon and had gone every night to the theatre. My hunger for the stage at that time was intense in a way I now find somewhat alarming. I watched plays with the kind of voracity with which small children read books; with the same visceral passion, the same complete trust in the imagination which is so difficult to sustain throughout the course of one's whole life. It sat uneasily with my daytime existence, spent in the luxurious squalor of dirty hotel bedrooms and the homes of affluent strangers.

There was one particular apartment, a place in St John's Wood, that spooked me from the moment I stepped into it, and I could never understand why. Having grown up in a fairly modest farming background I'd never before experienced such splendour, and I think I expected to be impressed. Instead of which, I fled every day when I had finished to a greasy-spoon café two streets away, where there was always a group of men off a building site, having their tea break. I grew to depend on them, on their yellow hats and their fag-smoke, their tabloids and their laughter. I don't think they ever noticed me sitting nearby as they ribbed each other and ate bacon rolls, swilling them down with big mugs of tea. The stifling atmosphere of the empty apartment where I worked felt like a parallel universe, and after a few hours there it did me good to be around the builders, to tap into their reality. All the rooms in the apartment seemed too big and were arranged in such a way as to militate against any kind of intimacy and warmth. They lacked such things as books and adequate light by which to read, an open fire or any sign of the presence of children; and no amount of Scandinavian glass, no number of cream sofas, could make up for this.

After I had been working there for about a fortnight, I turned around from the kitchen sink one afternoon and literally bumped into a young woman. Having believed myself to be completely alone in the flat it frightened me horribly, and I screamed so loudly that I frightened her and she screamed too. We both drew back and cowered, staring hard at each other like animals at bay.

Let's call her Lucy. That wasn't her real name, but it's what I called her when she became a character in my play. Over the following weeks a strange relationship developed between us that I mistakenly took to be a friendship. The manner of its conclusion proved how wrong I had been. Lucy was about three years younger than I, and had left school at the start of that summer. She hadn't applied to go to university and didn't know what she wanted to do with her life. Her boyfriend, she told me, was a film-maker and she was perhaps going to be a photographer, but she wasn't sure. The brother of a schoolfriend owned a photography gallery in the East End, and maybe she was going to have an exhibition there later in the year. Nowadays I would see through this kind of thing immediately; but this was the first occasion I had come across someone for whom art was a means of avoiding reality rather than confronting it head on, an idea so strange to me that I didn't fully comprehend it at the time. In some ways she was far more worldly and experienced than I – the film-maker boyfriend was only the most recent of many men – and then at other times she struck me as remarkably naïve and childlike, given her age. The one thing she craved was an audience, and I certainly provided *that* in due course. In the short term she trailed about the house in my wake as I polished and dusted, while she moaned about her mother and mimicked with little skill her father's mistress, whom she loathed. I came to realise how lonely she was, and how vulnerable. She adored her father, whose attention she could never hold for as long as she needed, and I grew to pity her. I only had to clean this palace of alienation; she, poor girl, had to live in it.

She insisted that I abandon my work for up to an hour at a time, to drink coffee with her and to talk about my life, for I was as exotic and interesting to her as she was to me. My childhood growing up on a farm in Northern Ireland fascinated her in a way I found hard to comprehend. I told her that I was the youngest of seven children. *I don't believe I've ever met anyone before with so many brothers and sisters.* That one of these brothers was a Catholic priest astounded her further. I described to her the wild boggy upland that was my home and my ambivalent feelings towards it. I thought she understood me. I thought she liked me. I thought she was my friend.

The summer ended and I prepared to go back to Dublin for my final year at college. Lucy wasn't in when I arrived at the apartment on my last day. I wanted to exchange addresses with her so that we could keep in touch. I thought to suggest to her that she would join me in the greasy spoon so that we could sit for a while in the reflected glow of the builders' camaraderie. It would do her good. I was in the kitchen when she did at last arrive home, bringing with her a young man. Whether or not it was the film-maker boyfriend or his successor I was never to know. 'I'll see you in a while,' she said to me, as she took him into the drawing room, which I had already cleaned. I hoped he wouldn't linger, but they sat there talking for the rest of the afternoon. At the end of my shift I put my head around the door.

'Well, what is it? What do you want?' Even I knew better than to suggest tea and bacon rolls at a moment like this.

'I've finished. I'm off now.'

'So, off you go.' I couldn't believe that all the time we had spent together, all our confidences, amounted to nothing.

'It's my last day!' I said helplessly.

'So, it's your last day.' She turned to the man and pulled a face, shook her little head, so much as to say, *You see the kind of people I have to put up with?* I withdrew from the room. As I was putting my jacket on in the hall I could hear him ask, 'Who was that?' and Lucy's reply, 'Oh it was nobody, it was just the cleaner. She's probably trying to scrounge a tip because it's her last day, but she's not getting anything.' I slammed the front door of the apartment behind me with all the force of Nora departing at the end of *A Doll's House*; and I kept this as the conclusion of *Summer with Lucy*: it was effective, even though it had been done before.

As soon as my finals were over at university, I took a job teaching English as a foreign language. All my classes were finished by lunchtime every day, and I spent my evenings and nights working on the play. I remember it as a time of great contentment. I wrote the play easily and quickly; I enjoyed doing it. I thought it would always be like this. I didn't know that forever after it would be a struggle to find the right words, the right form, that this sudden fluency was a gift, never to be repeated. If someone had told me this at the time, how would I have reacted? I'd probably have laughed at them. *Youth is wasted on the young.*

Summer with Lucy was a simple play, a two-hander, requiring a single set and providing two good roles for women. One of the characters was based on me; was a sharper, more witty and ironic me, someone whose *esprit* didn't wait until *l'escalier*. The other character was based on Lucy. I think I more than did her justice. I think I did her a favour. The 'real' Lucy was ultimately rather a dull girl, peevish and whingeing, with a distinct lack of imagination. I resented the choices and chances her wealth gave her and which she failed to realise. The Lucy I created was a far more complex personality, manipulative, intelligent, vulnerable and sly. The relationship she had with my fictional alter ego was edgier than it had been in real life, with a much stronger bond developing between the two characters and an underlying sense of violence. I knew when I finished it that I'd written a good play.

But I didn't realise just how good until it was accepted by Bread and Circus, the first company to which I sent it, and I attended the read-through.

Is there a more nerve-wracking, a more anxiety-inducing experience possible than first read-through? If so, I hope never to have to endure it. As an actor friend once remarked to me, 'It makes going on a blind date feel like yoga.' I think this is why I have no memory of actually meeting Molly, and this is something I very much regret. I can recall being there in the rehearsal room with her. 'It's so cold in here. Why is it always so cold? Does this thing work at all?' and she dragged the old gas heater across the floor, then hammered at the buttons on the side to try and switch it on. She helped me to a mug of bad coffee and asked me if I wanted milk. I was so nervous that I said no, even though I hate black coffee. All her initial conversation with me struck me as bland and oblique. I found her aloof. She chatted more with Ellen, the young woman who was to play 'my' character, and who, as a fellow member of the company, was an old friend of hers. I would like to be able to recall being introduced to her, the first words we addressed to each other, but in truth it's all lost now.

The read-through itself, though, remains vividly in my mind. Ellen was a fine actor, but Molly was outstanding. Even in that first raw attack on the text, she lifted the

19

whole thing to a new level. I had thought I knew every-thing – absolutely everything – there was to know about this play, which, after all, I and I alone had written. It was strange to realise that this was not the case. It was like being a composer and hearing the symphony one had, until then, heard only in one's mind, being suddenly played by a full orchestra, and being taken aback by its depth and resonance, far greater than one could ever have expected. In the course of the hour and a half that the read-through lasted, Molly became Lucy; and in doing so she reminded me, weirdly, of the real Lucy, of the lost and lonely child who had trailed around behind me in the apartment during that hot London summer.

As I have already said, I don't know how actors do what they do, so Molly's interpretation that day seemed almost magical to me, and yet I did wonder, as I was to wonder all through the weeks of rehearsal, what was the secret. It was only while watching her from the wings one night, months later, when the play was already a hit, that I realised one important part of the mystery. It was com-passion. Molly never judged a character. I had, at best, felt pity for Lucy, but Molly felt something more. No matter how difficult or unpleasant a character might seem, she could find in herself an understanding of why someone might be as they were and this enabled her to become them.

The read-through ended. Ellen brought the flat of her hand down hard on the table to represent the slamming of the door that ended the play and we all sat in silence for a few moments. Then Molly tossed her script down and threw her arms wide. 'We're all going to be famous!' she said.

It's the sort of foolish, camped-up and half-joking remark any ambitious young woman might make, but it was a memorable moment because she spoke no more than the truth. Within the year Molly, Ellen and I were if not exactly household names then certainly much talked about by anyone with even a passing interest in theatre. As soon as *Summer with Lucy* opened it became a word-of-mouth hit, a sensation. The first run sold out almost immediately, we revived it later that year in a bigger theatre with similar success. We took it to festivals both at home and abroad, and we all won awards. I was commissioned to write my second play; Molly and Ellen were courted with offers of prestigious roles; in short, we were on our way, launched with as much glory and honour as anyone could desire. Of the three of us, it was actually Ellen who became most famous with the general public in the long run. She moved into television work and made her name in a police drama watched by millions. On the day of the read-through she and the director had somewhere to go afterwards, and so it was to me alone that Molly said, 'Will we go and have a proper cup of coffee, instead of this sludge?'

At her suggestion, we went to the café where I had seen her sitting reading. 'I like this place,' she said artlessly, 'I come here all the time.' Our friendship began there on that day, and the café became a place to which we would often go together, or where we would arrange to meet. I found her much warmer than I had before the read-through, yet still she was reserved. At a nearby table someone had lit a cigarette, and the smoke drifted incessantly towards us. Molly fanned it away with her hand, but I could see that she found it increasingly irritating, until at last I said, 'Why don't I just go over and ask them to stub it out?' She looked at me with alarm. 'No, don't. They might get annoyed.'

'Well, their smoke's annoying us.'

She grasped my forearm to stop me moving. 'Don't, please don't. I can cope, really, it's not a problem.' She pleaded with me so vehemently that I felt I had no option but to do as she wished, and let the cigarette smoke drift on. But her behaviour puzzled me, and as we resumed our conversation, at the back of my mind I kept wondering about this. Suddenly it came to me. I knew it was the truth and yet it was a shock: *Molly Fox was shy*.

How could this be? I had seen her on stage only a few weeks earlier before more than a hundred people . . .

While I had been remembering all of this, drifting in and out of sleep, the radio had been idling. It was seven-thirty, the announcer now said, cutting into my thoughts. He read the news headlines with an air of incredulity, as if even he could hardly believe the horrors – political breakdown, hurricanes, house fires and car crashes – he was sharing with the nation. I rose and went to the bathroom, taking the radio with me. Even though here too Molly had urged me to make free with what was available, I didn't use any of her rose-scented bath oil in its bottle of smoked glass, the label hand-written in French. By the time I had washed and dressed the weather forecast was being read: it was to be a sunny day, warm and dry. I picked up the radio to take it down to the kitchen with me. I passed the door of the room where I had set up my computer and where I had been attempting to work in recent days. Enough: I could think of that later.

The stairs were carpeted with tough sea-grass and on the return stood a grandfather clock with a big pale face on which the name of the maker and the word *Dublin* was painted in a flowing hand; above this was a picture of the moon. The clock struck eight as I passed, dissonant against the pips of the radio. Then the newsreader gave the headlines again and more comprehensive details of the troubles of the world, which he still clearly found hard to believe. The usual scatter of letters was missing from the hall mat, reminding me again that it was Saturday.

In the kitchen I made coffee and toast, squeezed orange juice and boiled an egg. While waiting for it I set a tray, and when everything was ready I carried it out into the back garden. There was music again now. The piano had given way to contrapuntal singing, ancient and pure in high clear voices, evoking the grey cold of an empty cathedral, the shimmering light of a rose window. The back garden was much larger than the front, and quite different in its character. It was long, rectangular and confined by stout stone walls against which grew all manner of trailing plants: ivies and vines, sweet pea and climbing roses. There was a laburnum tree and beneath it metal chairs and a table topped with mosaic, where I settled down with the breakfast tray.

Near to the wall on the right-hand side was a row of fruit bushes, raspberries, gooseberries and blackcurrants. Molly told me she had planted these after reading a description in an estate agent's window of a house for sale 'with mature soft-fruit garden'. A more original and plausible come-on, we agreed, than 'fine, well proportioned rooms', or even 'paddock with own donkey', something that would be irresistible even to people who didn't know what a paddock was. And so even though she knew that what was meant was probably little more than a few tatty raspberry canes, a couple of mildewed currant bushes, she decided at once that she too would have to have such a thing. 'And until such time as they grow,' she had said, gesturing towards them, 'this is my *immature* soft-fruit garden. In the meantime, we can enjoy the raspberries.' *Raspberries*: she drew from the word all of its crushed and bleeding sweetness, its soft and jewelled redness.

At the other end of the garden there was a black-and-white cow. When I arrived at the house to stay some four days earlier Molly had still been there. As we stood talking in the kitchen while she made tea, I happened to glance out of the window and couldn't believe what I saw. Why was there a cow in her garden? How had it got there, given that the only ways in were either through the house or over the high stone walls? 'What is it?' she asked, for I had broken off in mid-sentence. She saw the look on my face and laughed. 'Don't worry, you're not the first to be taken in.'

The cow was made of fibreglass. Molly said she had seen it outside a junk shop and had known at once that she had to have it. 'Isn't it fabulous?' she said and she laughed again, staring out at the cow, her brown eyes shining and her whole face animated with delight. It was, I agreed. It was fabulous.

This was a lie. The fake cow was absurd, and it baffled and astonished me that Molly of all people should buy such a thing and put it in her garden. I mean, what was the *point* of it? Even a real cow seemed a more sensible, if less practical, idea. What bothered me most about this was that I had thought I knew Molly well. We had been friends for over twenty years now, and with the exception of Andrew, she was the last person I would have expected to go in for this type of whimsy. It was out of keeping with the style of the rest of the house, with its kilims and mirrors, its trays of beaten brass and low dark tables of solid wood. Sitting now at breakfast, staring at the cow, I wondered why I hadn't said this to her. I had always thought we knew each other well enough to be completely honest, at least about something as trivial as this.

I couldn't help wondering what Andrew would make of it. I have known Andrew ever since we were undergraduates together at Trinity. I was ostensibly reading for a degree in English Literature, but most of my time was taken up with student theatricals or sitting in my bedsit writing; for I was already determined to be a dramatist. My infrequent trips to the library were usually occasioned by a frantic need to study because of a deadline for an essay, or a tutorial paper to be prepared. Unlike some of my friends, I did not go there night after night to idle away my time: when I went to the library I really needed to get work done. I got into the habit of sitting in the Art History department because I knew I wouldn't meet any of my friends there and be distracted into wasting time in long whispered conversations. Art History also had the advantage of being nearer the exit than the English section, making it more convenient for the frequent coffee breaks that to me were essential.

I was aware of Andrew long before I spoke to him or knew who he was. I came to realise that no matter how early I went to the library (admittedly never that early) he was always there before me and at night he never left until the library closed. He habitually sat at the same desk. Surrounded by fortifications of books, great tomes on Romanesque architecture or medieval illuminations, he looked and had the air of a man under siege and toiled with a diligence at which I could only marvel. I remember that he had a silver fountain pen that he kept in a slim wooden box. He removed and replaced it with great ceremony – even then chipped and chewed biros would have been out of the question for Andrew. In time I came to like sitting near him because he created a force field of concentrated energy around himself into which one was drawn. I was less likely to daydream or doodle in the margins when under his influence. He also policed the area, and people who giggled or whispered would be ordered, in a marked Belfast accent, to stop. This was how I discovered that he was also from the north. He was tall and quite heavily built, with thick dark-blond hair that he would ruffle with his hands as he worked, so that by the end of most evenings he looked like a man who had had a bad fright.

'If you give me one of those cigarettes, I'll buy you a coffee.' He insists that those are the first words I ever spoke to him, although I can't remember it myself. It certainly sounds like me, and would tally with my idea that we first fell into conversation on a coffee break at the library doors. We came to acknowledge each other with a smile when I entered or left the library; we came to arrange our coffee breaks so that they coincided. I developed a Masonic gesture – the right hand held somewhat claw-like, the left closed but for an extended, slightly parted index and middle finger – to suggest it was time to stop for a drink and a smoke. He almost always accepted, and from time to time he would also accept one of the apples I usually had in my bag in those days, as an emergency food supply. But while I, once away from the books, would have been quite happy to sit chatting outside the library for the rest of the evening, Andrew would always look at his watch after exactly fifteen minutes and announce it was time for us to go back in.

What was he like then? I've already mentioned the Belfast accent, which was one of the most striking things about him. It disappeared so completely after he went to live in England that I'm still not convinced that he didn't take elocution lessons. I can detect a faint trace of it only occasionally on certain words or more generally when he's tired or angry. I doubt if anyone else would notice it at all, and I rather like it because it reminds me of the past.

Even then he wore his learning lightly and it was quite some time before I realised how quietly brilliant he was. Although he was from a modest background, he had attended a prestigious grammar school for boys to which he had won a scholarship. When I asked him why he had chosen to come to Dublin to study he said, 'To get away from Belfast, why d'you think?', but I subsequently discovered that he also had a scholarship to Trinity. While art history was his principal interest and was to remain a life-long passion, I discovered that he was also broadly interested in a great many other things, including history, music, philosophy, literature and drama. 'You have to be,' he said. 'Because they all fit together. There's no point in looking at them in isolation.' I think it's fair to say that I myself knew almost nothing in those days, and his well-stocked mind became a thing of wonder to me, as did the clarity and logic with which he expressed his ideas. This brilliance was the first thing that I understood about him.

Later, I realised that he was interested only in artifice. Nature meant nothing to him. It was as if the world around him were there solely to be translated into art. One afternoon, walking across Front Square together, I remarked upon the extraordinary clouds above us. He barely glanced up at them and made no comment. Then, remembering, brightening, he said, 'Constable did some amazing paintings of clouds; I must show you pictures of them.' A tree, a painting of a tree: he would always choose the painting.

One day he asked me, 'What was the first beautiful thing you ever saw?' I knew by then that to say 'A sunset' or 'A flower' was not what he meant, and that a fruit bowl my mother had made of green carnival glass wouldn't pass muster either, so I told him I had no idea. 'What about you?' I asked.

'It was the floor of a church, of all things,' he said with a laugh, 'which is ironic, given the way I feel about religion.' I knew by now that he had no time whatsoever for it. He told me that his parents had been infrequent churchgoers but that when he was about seven, he was taken out of school to visit the local church. 'I liked everything about it, to be honest – the coloured glass in the windows, the big brass eagle with a book on its outstretched wings, this strange-looking musical instrument, like a piano with loads of metal pipes coming out of it – I'd never seen an organ before, I didn't know what it was. But the floor was just gorgeous. I mean, now when I think of it, it was probably quite modest, but the colours –

terracotta, cream, bottle green, all in patterns and shiny. I hardly dared walk on it and I didn't want to leave at the end. The service itself didn't interest me, I just liked the building. That night, I was at home. We were having our tea and I was looking at the floor. It was covered in lino, grey with wee dark red squares scattered across it. I'd been looking at it all my life, but I realised then that it was ugly. I hadn't known until that day that a floor could be a thing so marvellous you couldn't take your eyes off it. And it didn't have to be in church. Sitting there I had a sudden revelation: that things could be beautiful or ugly and that practically everything in our house was ugly. The lino was ugly and the crockery was ugly, the curtains and the rugs, the bedding, and I hated it all. I wanted to live in a house where everything was beautiful. That was a good day. I knew from then on what I wanted.'

I soon realised that he didn't much care for the inhabitants of the ugly house, any more than he cared for its fixtures and fittings, and that he'd meant his early remark to me about studying in Dublin to get away from Belfast.

'My father works as a mechanic, my mother's a house-wife. I've one brother, Billy. He's three years older than me and he's an electrician. I don't really get on with him. We're not a close family; we don't have much in common.' We were outside the library, drinking coffee as usual and smoking when he told me this, and I was at something of a loss as to know what to say. I was aware it was a stupid question but I asked it anyway. 'What are your parents like?' Andrew narrowed his eyes and blew out a long stream of smoke. 'My mother's a snob. My father's a bigot. He would hate you – hate you – on principle. He'd call you a Papish. I must tell him some time that I'm good mates with someone whose brother's a Catholic priest. That'll be a laugh.'

'And Billy?'

Andrew's face closed. 'Don't even ask.' He dropped the butt of his cigarette into the dregs of his coffee. 'I'd best get back to the books.'

I was still very young then and I think I found it hard to imagine a family so unlike my own. My own background amazed Andrew, as it was to amaze Lucy and, in due course, a great many other people; and to begin with, this amazed me. At that time I thought my own family one of the most unremarkable there could be. I was the youngest of seven. The eldest was the priest, Fr Tom, and most of the siblings in between were already married with children of their own by the time I went to university. It all added up to a great warm web of people, sisters and brothers and husbands and wives, nieces and nephews, like some vast, complex soap opera but without the rows and the tension, without the violence and drama. They all still lived in the remote part of Northern Ireland where we had grown up and where my father worked a small farm. My family lived in scattered bungalows, or in semi-detached houses in estates at the edges of small market towns. They worked as teachers and as bank clerks, as nurses and minor civil servants. Two of my sisters stayed at home to look after their babies, and they helped mind the children of the other women in the family who went out to work. They all lived in each other's pockets, helping each other out, going to the pub together and to football matches, babysitting for each other, giving each other lifts here and there. At the time all this seemed perfectly normal to me. I was unaware that elsewhere in Western Europe, even in Ireland, the nuclear family was shrinking in on itself, as its emotional temperature plummeted.

Of all my brothers and sisters, I've always been closest to Tom, even though he's sixteen years older than me. Sometimes when we're all together again, at Christmas lunch or a family birthday, we'll look down the table at each other and suddenly connect. Over the shouting and roaring, the clash of cutlery and babies bawling, I see Tom and I as contained together in a private silence. Although we may not have what the others have, we know something that they don't. When I think of Tom, most often that's how I imagine him, smiling at me, complicit.

It was Tom who introduced me to the theatre. When I was twelve, he insisted, in the face of my mother's opposition, on taking me to Belfast to see *A Midsummer Night's Dream*. 'It'll be money down the drain. How could a child like that understand Shakespeare?' my mother said.

'She might, she might not,' was Tom's mild reply. 'At the very least it'll be an outing for her and company for me.'

In the car on the way to the city, he broadly outlined the story of the play, and this helped me to follow the action on stage. But my mother was right, there was much I didn't understand, and it was precisely this that drew me in. Certainly I was dazzled by the costumes and the lights, as any child might be, by the idea of actors and the whole strange world of the theatre. But it was the language that enchanted me most. I loved its blunt truth: *I am as ugly as a bear*, its richly visual quality, that called forth images even more vivid and real to me than the softly glittering scene before my eyes.

I know a bank whereon the wild thyme blows,
Where oxlips and the nodding violet grows

Afterwards, Tom loaned me his *Complete Works of Shakespeare*, with its Bible-fine pages. I looked up the text, these *words, words, words* that I had seen translated into the extraordinary experience of a few days earlier. Because even then I understood that theatre, if it was any good at all, wasn't something you saw, it was something that happened to you.

I knew that by this time I should go upstairs and get to work, but couldn't bring myself to do so. Instead, I made another cup of coffee and took it out to the back garden. The fake cow stared at me blankly. Molly had told me that there was a hedgehog living somewhere in the flower borders, much to her delight. 'Why are we always so pleased when we see a hedgehog?' she said. She had always thought of them as slow creatures, she told me, but that this one could move remarkably swiftly when it had a mind to do so.

One of the strange things about really old friendships is that the past is both important and not important. Taking the quality of the thing as a given – the affection, the trust – the fact that I had known both Molly and Andrew for over twenty years gave my relationships with them more weight and significance than friendships of, say, three or four years' standing. And yet we rarely spoke to each other of the past, of our lives and experiences during that long period of time. To do so would have been in many instances mortifying. Andrew once said to me, 'You have the most extraordinary memory,' to which I replied, 'I'm very good at forgetting things too,' and he responded, without missing a beat, 'I'm glad to hear it.'

During my first year at college, for example, I frequently went home at the weekends, because I still had a boyfriend in the north, someone with whom I had been going out since I was sixteen. Henry, his name was. He was studying in Belfast at the time; he was going to be a maths teacher. My family was extremely fond of him, and a significant part of those weekends home consisted of him sitting on our sofa with my nephews and nieces crawling all over him; or drinking cups of tea and talking to my brothers about hurling. 'Sounds like he's practically one of the family already,' Andrew said after I'd been talking to him about a recent visit. 'Your Ma probably thinks you're going to marry him.' Marry! Marry Henry, of all people! I actually laughed in Andrew's face when he said this, but, 'Think about it,' he replied. I did, later, and realised with horror (the word is not too strong here) that Andrew was correct. The pattern of my relationship with Henry was exactly that of my sisters when they had been going out with the men who were now their husbands, and there most probably was an unspoken understanding all round that we too would eventually get married and live locally. How could I not have seen it before now?

I dumped Henry suddenly, brutally, the following weekend. To be sure of a complete break I told him I'd been two-timing him for almost a whole term with someone in Dublin, and he was suitably, understandably, hurt. 'What's this man's name then?' he asked me coldly, and I almost spoiled it, almost blurted out, 'I don't know.' Henry's pain was nothing compared to my mother's anger. 'I don't know what kind of airs and graces you're getting about yourself at that university, madam, that the likes of Henry isn't good enough for you now. Leading him on like that, what must he think of us?' By Sunday night, my mother and I were barely speaking to each other.

Back in Dublin the following day, a look of alarm crossed Andrew's face when I told him what I'd done. 'It's nothing you said,' I hastily told him, which wasn't true, and 'It's a huge relief to me,' which was. And then, to my surprise, I began to cry, the first tears I'd shed over the whole affair. Andrew reacted with blokish unease in the first instance – lit me a cigarette, hadn't a clue what to say – but in the following days he consoled me. At his suggestion we went to a pub together one evening, something we hadn't done before. I told him I felt guilty about what had happened because I should have seen it coming. I had always known that I was something of a misfit in the family, but the visceral warmth, the fondness we all had for each other had prevented me from thinking through the nature of this difference, its implications. I knew instinctively the kind of life I needed to live, and since leaving home I had started to lead that life; I felt its rightness. But I hadn't realised until now that it would, inevitably, exclude me to some degree from my family, affection and love, even, notwithstanding.

'It's true,' Andrew said, 'you can't have it both ways.' He talked then about his own family, and was uncharacteristically forthcoming on the subject. 'It's indifference rather than hostility,' he said, 'although there's a fair bit of that too, particularly with my father. He's not a bit proud of me. When I do well in my studies, my exams, he takes it as some implied criticism of himself; he always has to get his dig in. Looking at pictures? Nice work if you can get it, although what's the bloody point? As for my mother, it's Billy who matters, not me.'

'What's he like?'

Now that I come to think of it, I have never heard any man mention his brother. The subject seems distasteful to most men.

'Billy? Billy's a hood. A wee smart-Alec and a hood, but my Ma thinks he's the be-all and the end-all. I had a big bust up with him about a month ago, the last time I was at home. I found a box under the stairs with a gun in it, a gun and ammunition.' He let me absorb this information for a moment, aware of how shocked I would be. This conversation was taking place in the early 1980s. Andrew and I were from opposite sides of a deeply divided society. Although we both abhorred the bitter sectarianism of that society we also knew that were we to talk about politics we were bound to disagree, to argue even. That's how deep the divisions went. Sometimes when I was back at home and I saw a tricolour flapping above the fields from a telegraph pole, or when one of my family members made a casual, bigoted remark for which they were rebuked by no one (including me, it has to be said), I did think of how ill at ease, how threatened, even, Andrew would feel on my turf, and with reason. Apart from the most oblique and passing references, we had until now dealt with the subject by the simple means of avoiding it. But one of those bullets Andrew had found could have had my father's name on it, my brother's, mine. To know that my friend had a brother who was a Loyalist paramilitary chilled me, and he knew this. It chilled him too, in a different way.

'I faced him with it and I argued with him.' I was just about to ask Andrew what he was going to do about it, and then I realised that I didn't want to know. 'I told my father as well but he already knew; I think he knows even more than he's letting on. He's worried, I can tell. Billy's in deep. Anyway,' he said, remembering the train of conversation that had brought him to this point, 'that's families for you, or at least that's my family. I'm stuck with them and they're stuck with me. Blood's thicker than water, I suppose.'

Does Andrew remember that night when we confided in each other, just after I broke Henry's heart? I'll never know, because were I to ask him, I'm sure he'd have the courtesy to pretend he had forgotten, unlike my mother who, to this day, casts Henry up to me. But it did mark a new stage in our friendship.

We never went to each other's houses, and for a long time college and a few selected pubs and cafés in the city centre remained our common ground. I didn't even know exactly where he lived until one day, in third year, when I had been bringing lecture notes to a friend in Rathmines who was ill and was afraid of falling behind with her work. God only knows what use my lecture notes would have been to anyone. Looking back it seems that everyone I knew at university was studying hard except me. It was late on a Saturday afternoon in winter, a bitterly cold day. Already the sun was beginning to set, a hard red that stained the few clouds pink and made the clear sky radiant, when I saw Andrew walking towards me, with great clusters of supermarket shopping bags dangling from his hooked fingers. We fell into conversation but almost immediately he suggested, because he was laden and because it was too cold to stand talking for long, that we go to his house, which was quite near. He was sharing a flat with two other students, in a house of faded elegance.

It had an imposing flight of steps and a fanlight over the door, but it also had four dustbins in the weedy front garden and a remarkable number of doorbells. 'With luck the others will be out,' he said as he turned the key in the lock, but there was a bike in the hall and we could hear the television blaring in the front room, and voices and laughter from the kitchen at the end of the hall. He frowned in annoyance, gestured with his head towards the stairs, and said 'Go up to my room; it's the one on the left. We'll have peace to talk there.'

His room faced west and was flooded with the livid pink light of the setting sun. It gave the place, indeed it gave the whole encounter that day, a curious atmosphere that makes the memory of it particular even now, some twenty years later. It was as though even as we were living it, it was already a little episode outside of time. I felt suddenly shy to be there and was glad he had told me to go upstairs first so that I could get used to being there in his room before he joined me. The room was exactly as I should have expected it to be, and every place where he has lived since then has had something of the same air to it, has been a place of scholarship and restrained aestheticism, the mirror of an ordered mind. Of course it has to be said that in other ways there is no compare, for his room then was the room of a student with very little money and his home now is the house of a rich and successful man.

I realise that a certain school of thought says that who we are is something we construct for ourselves. We build our self out of what we think we remember, what we believe to be true about our life; and the possessions we gather around us are supposedly a part of this, that we are, to some extent, what we own. I have always been, and still am, hugely resistant to these ideas, because, I think, they are so much at odds with the Catholic idea of the self with which I was raised. I still believe that there is something greater than all our delusions about ourselves, all our material bits and pieces, and that this is where the self resides. But if anyone can give me pause in this argument, it's Andrew, the most patently and successfully self-constructed person I have ever met.

His room, on that winter afternoon so long ago, had a curious air of stillness because of the pink light. The high windows were uncurtained. The most evident piece of furniture was the desk which, like the desk he usually occupied in the college library, was stacked high with books about fine art. His precious fountain pen was there too in its wooden box. A drinking glass held other pens and pencils; there was an angled desk lamp with a cream shade. The single bed, with its dark red paisley spread, seemed to be masquerading as a couch by day. There were three chairs, one a battered but comfortable looking armchair, the others hard kitchen chairs, one of which was at the desk; the other had been pressed into service as a bedside table. A fire had been set with sticks and twisted newspapers in a small iron grate that I supposed was original to the house. There were coloured tiles showing stylised flowers along the sides of the fireplace, and a bale of turf briquettes stacked neatly alongside it. The whole room was neat and tidy, staggeringly so, when I thought of the way my brothers had kept their rooms, my benchmark then for the domestic arrangements of young men and not, I think, untypical. What made it more surprising still was that Andrew had not been expecting callers. I doubted that I could have brought my own abode to this degree of order even with a few days' notice. Beside the wardrobe, a poor piece of workmanship, was a row of shoes, and looking at them I was struck by the strange pathos of someone's possessions when the person themselves is absent.

I wandered around the room while I waited for him, examining the spines of the books in his little bookcase, then crossing to the desk where a textbook lay open. On facing pages were black-and-white photographs of the facades of two cathedrals, Chartres and Amiens, and I wondered how he made sense of them. I would have had nothing to say about those dense concentric arcs of stone carvings, all those thickly crowded angels and saints; it would have bored me even to think about it. With that, Andrew came into the room. 'I should have told you to light the fire.' He set down the tray of coffee and biscuits he was carrying and knelt down, lit the paper. Quietly it took, then the fire-lighters concealed beneath the sticks caught and we both stared at the licking flames, as the wood crackled. 'You have no curtains,' I remarked, and he looked up at the window as if he were only noticing this now. 'I took them down. Horrible Seventies things – sort of big brown swirls with orange blobs. Couldn't live with them and anyway, I like the light in the morning. Wardrobe's rubbish too but what can you do?'

As he spoke he started to build a small wigwam of briquettes over the flames, and then he stood up and switched on the desk lamp. The sky was growing darker, but because of the lamp and the flames of the firelight, the light in the room was still peculiar in a way I loved. I found myself wishing it could stay like that, in the foolish way I had wished for things when I was a child. For I wanted the night not to come, I wanted this peaceful stillness, illuminated so perfectly, to go on and on. I think I could understand then why he liked certain paintings so much, for that closed, perfected world that they offered. He asked if I wanted him to put on some music and I said no, I was happy with things as they were. We sat for a while in companionable silence, watching the flames of the fire. He lived on a quiet side street, and from time to time we could hear buses and cars rumble past on the main road out from the city.

He told me that he was going to a party that night. Any impression I may have given of a dour introvert is wholly inaccurate. Andrew was an aesthete but not an ascetic. He liked a party or a pint as much as many another; and he had his own circle of friends, people who happened not to be friends of mine. He also had an essay to write, and was planning to spend the Sunday working on it. I told him frankly that I didn't know how he endured his studies, but instead of becoming defensive or annoyed he seemed to relish the challenge of sharing his enthusiasm. 'Let me show you just how interesting it can be.'

He selected a book from the pile on his desk and leafed through it, found the painting he required. It was an Annunciation, a simple image, deceptively simple I realised, as he talked me through it. He explained the iconography and the composition, how things were harmoniously arranged in a way of which the viewer was not immediately conscious, but which subtly made their effect nonetheless. He told me something of the biography of the painter, his place in the art of his time. In spite of myself I became fascinated, and I could see how much

Andrew was enjoying himself too. Now that he is regularly on television, teaching people about art with the same easy brilliance, it pleases me to think that I was his first pupil. We drank the coffee and smoked, sat by the fire together for an hour and more. It was a happy afternoon, and when I was leaving I told him to have a good time at the party. I hope he did. Although neither of us knew it at the time he needed a little bulwark of pleasure in his life to set against what was about to befall him two days later.

I slept in for my nine-o'clock lecture on Monday and was bumbling around the kitchen, still in my dressing gown, when the phone rang. As soon as Andrew spoke I knew by the sound of his voice that something was seriously wrong. He asked me if I had heard the news headlines that morning and I said that I had. 'That man,' he said, 'the man who was shot, the body they found on the mountain – that was Billy.'

I'm ashamed to say that this murder had barely registered with me when I'd heard it on the radio, for such events were a commonplace in Northern Ireland in the 1970s and '80s. One became numb to them and only became aware of the full creeping horror when, as now, there was a personal connection. Andrew told me that Billy's name would be released later that day and that he was ringing his friends so that they wouldn't learn of it first through the media. He rightly scoffed at my suggestion that I might go to Belfast for the funeral. Two days later I saw a report of it on the television news. I glimpsed Andrew emerging from a tiny redbrick house, supporting his mother, with his head bowed. Billy had been murdered as part of a Loyalist paramilitary feud. He had been abducted on the Saturday night and shot, his body

41

dumped on the mountains above the city, where it was found late on the Sunday night.

What shocked me most when Andrew returned to college the following week was not his sorrow but his anger. He was full of a rage he could just about keep under control and he brushed aside my condolences with a sardonic laugh. I wasn't hurt, for I understood how complex and poisoned his grief must be for his only brother who had also been his rival, his enemy; and whose murder had made his own situation within his family even more painful than it already was. He didn't speak of it, how could he? He became more absorbed in his studies than ever before.

All this came back to me as I sat in Molly's garden on the morning of her birthday over the ruins of breakfast; over the broken eggshell in its cheery little egg-cup, a thing such as a child might like, made of thick pottery with the name *Molly* painted on it in primary colours. The speckled light came down through the leaves of the trees and trembled on the table top. The morning was moving along but I wasn't moving with it. I would have been happy to sit there for at least another hour just thinking about the past, but I knew that if I let more time slip away, I would regret it later. I carried the breakfast tray into the house and started to tidy up. As I did the dishes I glanced from time to time out into the garden, at the raspberry canes and the shaded table, at that ridiculous fake cow. Being in the house was the next best thing to being with Molly herself. She loves her home with an extraordinary kind of psychic intensity, and her whole sense of self, her identity, is intimately bound up with it in a way I had thought only possible when a house had been in a family for generations. That sense of gratitude to the dead who had planted those trees, those roses, who had chosen those possessions, simple perhaps – the floral plates that have been in the back of the cupboard time out of mind, those plain white candlesticks – gratitude and a sense of obligation to the future: there is none of that here. All of this is Molly's choice and her creation, and she inhabits this space so fully that as I stood there with my hands in the hot suds I suddenly felt that she was there with me, even though I knew that this was impossible, that she was in New York. I sensed Molly's spiritual presence as completely as I had failed to sense Lucy's physical presence in that London apartment all those years ago, so much so that I turned away from the sink and looked behind me.

There was nobody there, of course. There was only the kitchen table where Molly and I had sat together for so many hours over all the years we had known each other. It was at this table that she had first told me about her family. Her mother had been absent from her life since very early on, although she was vague and elusive as to why that should have been the case. She had one sibling, a younger brother named Fergus, who threw a great shadow over her life and was a constant source of worry. Fergus was helpless where she was capable, was a failure where she had succeeded. When she talked of these things her voice, that beautiful voice, changed and she spoke in a way I never heard her speak otherwise, neither privately nor on stage. It was as if she had a special register, a tone that she kept for this subject and for this alone. 'Oh Molly!' I said once, for I was at a loss as to know how to respond to what I was hearing. 'Don't pity me,' she replied and her tone was sharp. 'All I want is to be an actor and to have a home and I've got both of those things. I've got everything I want.'

I rinsed the last plate and put it on the drainer, made myself more coffee in a china mug speckled with polka dots. The big clock at the head of the stairs bonged softly for nine-thirty. I carried the mug out of the kitchen, into the hall and through to the sitting room. It looked this morning like some kind of jewelled casket, like a box of treasures. Sunlight caught on copper and brass, was reflected in polished wood and in mirrors. All this glitter and brightness was offset by the rich dark colours of the kilims on the floor.

The whole room was crammed with books, both in open bookshelves built into the walls and in a free-standing antique bookcase with glass doors. This latter holds her most precious books, for Molly is a bibliophile as well as a reader. For many years now she has bought herself a book to celebrate and mark each role she has played. Inside each one is a small white card on which she has written the details of her part in the production which that book honours, the date and the name of the theatre. Some of them are editions of the plays concerned. The earliest ones, from when she was starting out and had very little money, are simply good hardback editions of favourite works; but the most recent ones are rare and valuable books, including signed copies and first editions, many with fine bindings. Some have stiff ridges on the spines, others are supple in soft leather, with the edges of the fine pages gilded. Many of the bindings are stamped in gold, with patterns of vines and little birds, flowers and acorns. She has a lot of Shakespeare on these shelves, the complete works several times over and many individual plays as well. There are also quite a few contemporary works, including many of my own plays, with written dedications to her from me. Looking at the spines of these books now brought back times we had worked together.

Molly has been something of a muse to me over the years. The best roles I have written for women have been created with Molly in mind. Our gifts complement each other in a way that is, I believe, rare. Often when I am writing for her I can hear her voice. Sometimes it is so clear it is as if she is speaking aloud, as if she were there in the room with me. It becomes an uncanny thing, almost occult. It gives me confidence and courage to know that I have such an instrument at my disposal. I would not be the writer I am without Molly. She can find the depth charge in the most apparently simple language. Once, when we were talking about Shakespeare, she remarked to me that the most seemingly simple and straightforward lines were the most potent, and also the most difficult for an actor to deliver. The richest and most complex language was the easiest.

The barge she sat in, like a burnish'd throne
Burned on the water; the poop was beaten gold,
Purple the sails . . .

The poetry was already there, all one had to do was speak it. But:

To take is not to give.
What! In our house?
I am the sea.

To bring out the complex meaning, all the possibilities of words such as these, was the great challenge for an actor.

Just before she left for New York, she had opened the bookcase and showed me her latest acquisition, bought to mark her triumph at the start of that year in *The Duchess of Malfi*. As long as I have known her she has hungered after the role of the Duchess. I had never understood this and had told her so. I found the play absurd, Grand Guignol, too over the top to be taken seriously, with its poisoned, violent atmosphere. I had had the misfortune to see a bad production of it early in my career, and that, understandably, had put me off. At Molly's insistence I read the text, which struck me as frankly daft. It's a classic Jacobean tragedy. The Duchess of the title is a widow. She has two brothers, the Cardinal, whose evil is icy, and the mad Duke Ferdinand, who harbours incestuous feelings towards her. Against their wishes, she remarries, in secret. The brothers get wind of what has happened and all kinds of horrors follow on as a result: stranglings, murder by poisoned Bible, a parade of madmen, a severed hand.

Molly insisted that were I to see it performed in a good production, I would change my mind. She said it was one of those plays that are, yes, silly on the page, but can be transformed by the alchemy of the stage into something deeply affecting. She pointed out to me, as if I needed reminding, the difference between the text and what it might become. While Shakespeare or Chekhov might afford some of the most sublime theatre one might ever experience, they were also likely, Molly argued, to be behind some of the deadliest, most numbingly tedious performances imaginable. Her arguments were so persuasive that I read the text again. Slowly I began to see what she was getting at. There were things about the play that were curious and seemed contradictory. The overall effect was suffocating and overheated. It was complex and corrupt, shot through with the knowledge of pure evil. All the acts perpetrated in it were acts of darkness. And yet these effects were achieved, as Molly pointed out to me, through language of extraordinary clarity, simplicity and power. *Look you, the stars shine still.*

Over the years, this wish of hers to play the Duchess would be mentioned occasionally in interviews as the one particular thing that she still wanted to do, hoping, I suppose, that some director would read the interview and take the bait. As she moved into her mid-to-late thirties we both knew that time was running out. Like most female actors Molly is both cagey and touchy about her age, and with good reason. Knowing that she is unlikely to be cast below her real age, she takes care to not let it be known what age she is. When she was finally offered the role of the Duchess my happiness for her was tempered by the fear that as with so many things for which one longs for years, it would prove to be a disappointment.

The book she had shown me, and which I now lifted from the shelves to examine again more closely, had been commissioned from a bookbinder. It was the play itself bound in black velvet and red silk, with the title stamped in red metal foil on the spine. Molly herself had suggested the design, and had been thrilled with the final result, with this erotic, dangerous-looking little volume that I held in my hands. When she was showing me the books she had urged me not to be precious about them, had insisted that although they were rare and remarkable objects they were still books and were there to be read. Reading is one of the great pleasures, the great necessities of her life. *Take them and read them, use them, enjoy them. That's what they're there for.*

Yes, Molly loves reading, more than anyone else I know, and she has plenty of time for it because her emotional life takes up no time at all. *I'm only really interested in casual relationships. Cream off the best of someone and then move on. Anything else is a waste of time.* I was shocked when she said this to me not long after we first met, when I was still young and relatively inexperienced myself. It made me feel uneasy about my new friend, but I consoled myself by thinking that it was all bravado, she didn't really mean it. Time taught me that she did. In all the years I've known her she has never been in a serious long-term relationship, nor with anyone about whom I felt she cared deeply. Given her charm, her status, her extraordinary gift, there is never any lack of men keen to be with Molly Fox. Although she helped me through the two major break-ups in my life, first with Ken and then with Louis, and did so with all the kindness and compassion one could wish for, I couldn't help wondering if, deep down, she thought me ridiculous for taking it all so much to heart.

Ken was an actor, and some years after *Summer with Lucy* I met him in the same way as I met Molly, when he was in a play I'd written. This time there were roles for one woman, which had been written with Molly in mind, and two men. I was happy with the director's casting of Ken, whom I knew by reputation to be a serious actor, and who struck me as perfect for the part. Initially I was extremely resistant to the choice of the third actor, David McKenzie, but I let myself be persuaded by Ken and the director, both of whom had worked with him before.

If I don't remember the moment I met Molly, I certainly remember, with cinematic clarity, the moment I met David. He was sitting with his back to me and turned around as I came into the room. I thought I'd never in my life seen so handsome a man. He held out his hand and he smiled at me, he said my name, and I knew for certain that I'd never in my life seen so handsome a man. He was dark-haired, with perfectly regular features, but two things transformed these rather standard good looks into something exceptional. Firstly, he had green eyes, as close to the green of a cat's eye as I have ever seen on a human being, but warm, unlike a cat's, beguiling. The other thing was the sheer force of his personality.

One of the reasons I hadn't wanted to work with David was that I had read several interviews with him and they had put me off. They all insisted breathlessly how delightful and friendly, how kind and good-humoured, how *nice* he was; and of course I hadn't believed a word of it. He was an actor, for goodness' sake; he could become whatever he wanted to be so as to appear favourably in the eyes of those around him. I suspected that under all the charm there was probably a cold and manipulative person. On meeting him myself, however, all of this was immediately forgotten. His was an energising presence, happy and uncomplicated, decent and warm. He was funny – not witty, wit was beyond him – but funny in the engaging, slightly silly way a small child can be funny. Above all he operated like a strange kind of mirror, so that you saw his many strengths and virtues reflected in yourself. By being attractive he made you feel attractive, by being sincere, sincere. Taken all together, the looks, the charisma and those green eyes, it was quite a package. I'm neither ashamed nor embarrassed to admit that I was completely dazzled by him. He was at that time twenty-five, a few years younger than Molly and me, and had recently married a woman named Mel with whom he'd gone to school. He was becoming much talked about as an actor; there was a sense that he was on the cusp of great things. It was an exceptionally good moment in his life.

He did have a name for not being the most intelligent man in the world, something he brought up himself on that first day and didn't deny. 'I hope you're not going to ask me about my theory of acting or anything,' he said to me. 'I don't know how to talk about it, I just sort of do it.' Why, that wasn't a problem at all, I told him; that made perfect sense: he just sort of did it. Once I was out of the force field of his allure, however, I did begin to worry, because intelligence is something I particularly appreciate in an actor. It comes through in performance, but it's important in rehearsal too. If David failed to see what was required of him, would it be possible to explain to him? Would he understand?

Working with him, then, was a revelation. David was a deeply instinctive actor, more so than anyone I had known up to that point in my career or indeed in the years since then. He was a gift to any writer because, not having the wherewithal to question a text, he trusted it implicitly. He took a play at face value and went straight to the heart of it. His innate understanding of any given role more than made up for any lack of conscious knowledge and the inability to explain what he was about. It simply didn't matter. 'It's like footballing intelligence,' Ken remarked to me one day as we watched Molly and

David rehearsing a scene together. 'All that counts is that you can put the ball in the back of the net. Whether or not you can explain afterwards how you did it is neither here nor there.'

Ah yes, Ken. I became very close to him very quickly, and we were a couple by the time the play went up. There was a kind of perfection about that period in our lives. We all brought out the best in each other, both professionally and personally. Molly and David hit it off particularly well in spite of their being so different. He had none of her emotional complexity, her depth; and she was happy to let his sunny good nature set the tone. It was an invigorating experience, that production, in spite of the play itself being so dark. Contrary to popular belief, the spirit abroad in the rehearsal room does not necessarily mirror the genre of the play in question. Working on a comedy can be a fractious, ill-tempered affair; and Molly claims she has never laughed so much as when she was rehearsing *Phèdre*. We got great reviews and the run was extended. I never worked with David again after that, more's the pity.

I did work again with Ken, and that's a pity too, because it ruined what there was between us personally. We were together for a few years and I almost married him, but the more intimate we became the more professional rancour came between us. It was I who, like a fool, insisted that we work together once more. Ken knew that it was a mistake but I forced him into it. I couldn't see until it was too late that even given the circumstances of our initial meeting and it having been a good experience, it could never be like that again. Other people now saw us as a couple. To disagree with one was to risk upsetting both; and for Ken to disagree with me before other people was something I couldn't handle; I took it personally. All kinds of resentments and rivalries infested our life together and eventually brought our relationship to an end. And it was all my fault.

I stood there in the morning light with Molly's copy of *The Duchess of Malfi* in my hands. Why was I remembering all of this now? It was all so long ago, but it was still painful to think of it. As I replaced the book I noticed a volume of Chekhov short stories, and in spite of myself I lifted it out to look at it. Before I knew what had happened I was on a jetty in Yalta, then the clock on the stairs was sounding ten o'clock and the untouched coffee was cold beside me in the polka-dot mug. In my defence I must say that this was most unlike me. Usually I am a most disciplined writer. When I am at home writing I don't stop when I hear the clatter of the letter box and the soft tumble of the post on the mat. I hear the click of the answering machine in the next room and I give little thought to who it might be. I do not procrastinate, I do not waste time. These mornings in Molly's house were exceptional in this way, and if I was going to do anything at all today I would have to start now. I left the cold coffee where it was and went upstairs.

I spent what was left of the morning working, that is to say, given that it was the early stages of a new project, that I spent the morning wool-gathering, staring out of the window into the back garden, reading over my notebooks, writing things down and then crossing them out again moments later; and all the time thinking about the man with the hare.

Some years earlier I had been on a tram in Munich when I noticed that a man standing near to me was holding in his arms what I at first took to be a large rabbit and then realised was a hare. The man, who was in his forties, was wearing a brown flecked jumper with a hole in the elbow and a ravelled cuff. He was unshaven and looked tired; I remember that the knuckles of his right hand were skinned raw. He was holding the hare cuddled to his chest as one might carry a baby, and it concealed most of the upper part of his body, for the creature was massive. Apart from its size, the thing that struck me most about it were its strange ears, folded along the length of its back, and the curious shape of its head. The skull looked as if it had been crushed, and had a big brown eye on either side. It made me think of tropical fishes, as flat as coins, and I wondered what its field of vision must be. Its fur was mottled and neutral, so that it blended in with the colour of the man's jumper. I could understand how in its natural habitat – in open bogland, for instance – it would be superbly camouflaged, even when it was moving. It carried to the heart of the city a sense of wild places, of exposed moorland where there was heather but no trees, where there were small dark reedy lakes swept by the wind and rain. It reminded me of home. The hare was completely still in the man's arms. At no point did it attempt to struggle or wriggle, and they were both still on the tram when I got out at Marienplatz.

I knew that the man and the hare were the trigger for the play that I was going to write. That is not to say that it would be about them. They would not appear in it, would in all likelihood not be described or even mentioned. But I knew that by going through them, by grasping imaginatively something about them, I would be able to get at what I needed to know and then I would be able to write the play.

This had been going on for several weeks now, and a kind of panic was beginning to settle on me. I tried not to think too much about the fact that this would be my twentieth play, for it gave me no comfort. Sitting at Molly's desk, there were times when I felt I had never before written a line in my life, and the idea of my producing a work that any professional company would wish to stage struck me as an absurdity. My past experience counted for nothing. This feeling was in itself a normal part of the process of writing: I knew this. I also knew that for the act of writing to become increasingly difficult rather than easier with each work was logical. It would have been easy to repeat things that had been successful, to slip into stale and formulaic writing. But I wanted every time to do something new, something that would surprise the public, something that would perhaps surprise even me. I wanted to do something of which I hadn't, until then, known I was capable. And this too was a normal part of the process. While it sometimes got me down, it was also usually what got me out of bed in the morning. It was a challenge, and I loved it.

No, there was a particular reason why getting to grips with my twentieth play was such a struggle and it was this: my nineteenth had been an unprecedented disaster.

Looking back on it now – something I still try to avoid – it appears to me as an accursed inversion, as a reflection in a dark mirror, of having my first play produced. Then I had found in Molly, the leading actor, a friend for life. In the director of my most recent work, I had made a mortal enemy who I felt was probably still poisoning my reputation about the place, even as I sat there, gazing down at the fake cow. I had written *Summer with Lucy* in a headlong rush of confidence, certain of what I was about. Nothing before or since had come so easily to me; at times it had been like taking dictation. My only problem had been to keep up with the flood of dialogue and incident that rushed through my mind, day after day.

Halfway through writing *The Yellow Roses* I fell ill. It was quite serious and lasted several months, leaving me drained and devitalised. When I was finally well enough to start work again, I found I had lost all interest in the play; but because of the time and effort I had already invested in it, and for want of another immediate project, I felt I had to at least try to crank up some enthusiasm and keep going. Although I was heartily sick of it by the time I finished it, it was, I still believe, a fine play, as good as anything I've written, or I would never have delivered it for production. Indeed at that stage the signs were all positive, and I thought that my luck had turned. The text was well received by those who read it, and I was surprised and delighted when Stuart Ferguson said he wanted to direct it.

Stuart was the latest theatrical marvel. When barely out of college he directed a stunning *Medea* – I had seen it myself – that had made his name. He followed this with outstanding productions of *The Cherry Orchard* and *Measure for Measure* and then a successful film; and all this was accomplished well before his thirtieth birthday. My play was to be the first contemporary work he had tackled for the stage. Our initial meeting, over coffee in a central London hotel, was perfectly cordial, with much mutual admiration expressed. What I had seen of his work had greatly impressed me. He was clearly keen to direct the play, and what he said to me about it made me believe that he had grasped its central idea, that he understood it. But after we had shaken hands and I walked off through the wet grey streets of a London dusk, under all my relief at having found a gifted director for my new play there was, I knew, something unwanted and unpleasant, hard and dry as a pip: dislike. I didn't like Stuart and I suspected that he didn't much like me.

I have asked myself many times since that day why, so late in my professional life, did I make such a basic mistake as to go against my instincts, to ignore Dislike (ignoring, too, Dislike's sinister little brother, Distrust). My illness and the subsequent struggle to complete *The Yellow Roses* had unnerved me. I was rattled, worn out. I needed the energy and confidence, the charmed magic of success that I didn't feel in myself but that I believed Stuart could bring to the production. In this I was forgetting about my own considerable reputation which was, I suppose, why Stuart swallowed his own dislike of me and wanted to direct the play.

I found him false. His origins were not dissimilar to my own. We both came from modest farming backgrounds, in a remote boggy part of Tyrone, mountainous and wild, in my case; a croft in the Scottish highlands in his. Stuart held the world that had produced him in contempt. Apart from the accent, which he'd decided to keep, he'd made himself over completely. In itself, I wouldn't have had a problem with this. Andrew had done the same thing and I'd found it admirable. The difference was that with

Andrew I always felt that he had become something he needed to be, something that he was but that had been denied to him until he had the courage to accept it. Stuart was just a phoney.

For all that, agreement was reached, dates fixed, actors cast and contracts signed: Stuart and I were locked into working together. Molly thought that a certain degree of tension between us might be no bad thing. She told me that she had on occasion done good work with people she didn't much care for, whom she'd found abrasive or hostile. Even if it was dark energy that was being generated it was still energy, and if it could be converted and channelled into the work it would make for a powerful production. 'You're not going to live with this person,' she pointed out. 'You don't have to be their friend.' Her argument persuaded me, because I realised that I had experienced the opposite situation many years earlier, when a cast, director and technical people had been so fond of each other, such good mates and so uncritically admiring of each other's efforts, that the end result had had all the edge and power of a school play.

And so we went into rehearsal. *The Yellow Roses* was about an Irish couple, Ellie and Lorcan, who had moved to London in their twenties, she a nurse, he a labourer, where they met and married. Now in retirement, Lorcan wants to go back to live in Connemara again, while Ellie insists she wants to stay in London. The conflict between them about this, together with the input from their doctor daughter and schoolteacher son, formed the substance of the play. It was a work that dealt with the nature of home, how it was often a state of mind as much as a place.

After I left my family to go to university, I never again lived in the north, but it has remained a constant in my life, a touchstone, the imaginative source of so much of my writing. Even this new play I was struggling now to write in Molly's house was connected with it: the hare's world was also mine. I have always believed that I know who I am, no small thing in the shifting dream that is contemporary life. I put this down to my background, my identity as solid as the mountainside on which I grew up. With Stuart and the actors we talked in rehearsal about home, about returning. I said that the person in the play with whom I most closely identified was Lorcan. I told them that although I too had lived in London for most of my adult life my plan was that eventually I would live in Ireland again.

'But you can't,' Stuart said. 'You can never go back. Never' – and when I gently protested against this, he became more vehement, scornful even. Our discussion quickly moved from being a valid exploration of something to help us in the production of the play to personal acrimony. I suppose I had known that going back was as much a wish as a plan, and writing the play had been a way for me to deal with it, to let myself down gently. I knew Stuart was probably right, and he knew that I knew, that was the worst thing. 'And anyway, why would you want to go back?'

'I do!' I cried, petulant as a child. 'I just do!' He laughed and turned away, changed the subject. He'd rattled me in front of the cast, got under my skin, and I realised then that this was how he operated.

In the following days and weeks he worked his way steadily through everyone involved in the production, systematically sowing conflict and dissent, setting people up and playing them off against each other. By instilling a sense of fear and insecurity in everyone, he wanted to get the upper hand. I could see how this tactic might work. Doubtless it had contributed to his rapid rise and early successes; but to deliberately create tension and unease in an enterprise as fragile as a theatre production is a high-risk strategy, and on *The Yellow Roses* his luck ran out. We all eventually realised that he was an arch manipulator, but by then the damage had been done.

I remember watching him the night before the first preview as he berated the young actor who was playing the daughter. Had this happened early in rehearsal I would have got involved myself and tried to get him to back off. Now I realised that this was exactly what he wanted and that I would most likely have ended up arguing with the actor while Stuart withdrew, amused and in control. I kept my own counsel and studied him from the far side of the room. His accent, the expensive casual clothes he wore, the small leather-bound books in which he made notes while he worked and the black fountain pen with which he made them: all of this I held in disdain. What was he running away from? I asked myself. And what did he think he was running towards? I loathed social ambition as much as I approved of artistic ambition, of making the work as good as it could possibly be; and Stuart was a shameless social climber, always dropping names, always sucking up to the famous and powerful.

By the time the first night came, I thought that if *Summer with Lucy* had been the glorious start to my career then *The Yellow Roses* might well mark its ignominious end. I couldn't help hoping for a miracle, of the kind that does sometimes happen in the theatre. Was it possible that all the ill-will generated, all the bad feeling rife in the company, might by some strange means be converted into that good energy of which Molly had spoken, that it might transform and electrify the production?

No. There was to be no miracle. The first night did not go well and we all got mauled in the press the following day, every last one of us: the cast, the set designer, the wardrobe people, the musicians; but the most scathing and dismissive responses were aimed at the writer and the director. I read the reviews the following morning with that strange, flesh-crawling sensation, that sudden brief flush of a chill, nauseous feeling that goes with being on the receiving end of a bad press. *This tedious play . . . lacklustre production . . . yellow roses that have faded and lost their bloom . . . banality . . . inept . . . truly dreadful . . .* It was like being mugged. By some weird means the critics divined the bad feeling between Stuart and myself and cranked it up. *There's no knowing what possessed Stuart Ferguson to make his contemporary directing debut with this lazy play, from a writer whose best work is long past.* Lazy? Christ Almighty! Now I was ready to mug the mugger. I pushed the newspapers away from me and with that the phone rang.

'You must be bitterly disappointed.' It was Molly. That marvellous voice was charged with all the power that those two words were capable of carrying, the bitterness, the disappointment, and yet to hear it made me feel better, as if she was able to articulate for me the pain that I could only feel. 'Yes, Molly,' I said, 'I am.'

Perhaps the most unfortunate thing of all was that my ignominy coincided exactly with her greatest triumph.

She had opened in *The Duchess of Malfi* a fortnight earlier, and already it was being called a performance that would define the role for a generation. If my play had also been a success, how we would have celebrated together! If I had been as I was now, quietly engaged in writing a new work, I would have been energised and fired up by her success. Instead, we both had to face at the end of that week a newspaper column giving an overview of current theatrical offerings:

> *Don't Miss: Molly Fox is a magisterial Duchess of Malfi.*
>
> *Don't Bother: The Yellow Roses: Tedious and turgid.*

I realised immediately that this would be every bit as painful and unpleasant for Molly as it was for me. It gave, and then it took away. Our friendship and our close artistic collaboration on many of my plays were common knowledge. It was as if she was being used to humiliate me. Even Molly has had bad notices in her day, and if a performance of hers had been rubbished in the same breath as my work was being praised, it would have killed off any pleasure I might have felt; it would have enraged me. But I couldn't find the words to say all this to Molly.

All this had happened at the start of the year, and now it was midsummer. Now I was sitting in a spare bedroom in Molly's house, gazing down into her garden and trying to write a new play. Now I was beginning to realise how severely damaged my confidence had been by all of this. As I sat at the desk, struggling with the idea of the man and the hare, I couldn't help wondering if I was unconsciously trying to close down my own imagination, so that I wouldn't be able to write another play, and as a result would never have to go through such a grisly experience again. My computer screen had gone black yet again, as coloured geometric shapes morphed languidly across it. I moved the mouse just for the sake of it, to cancel the screen saver and bring up what little text was there, to give myself the illusion of actually doing something. As one does in such circumstances I tried to find an excuse, and decided it was to do with the room in which I was working.

It had been Molly's idea that I sleep in her bed and set up my computer in the de facto spare room. There were white gauze curtains figured with daisies. When I stayed with her in winter, Molly always lit a fire for me in the tiny fireplace. The bed had a pink quilt and was piled with small lacy pillows. There was the desk and chair at which I was working and a comfortable chintzy armchair. It was soft and bright and restful.

Once, many years ago, not long after I first met Molly and a short while after she'd bought the house, I came at her invitation to spend a day with her. When she met me at the door she looked thoughtful and concerned. 'Fergus, my brother, is staying here with me,' she said. 'He's had a kind of breakdown.' She didn't elaborate and I didn't pursue the matter. I had never met Fergus. He was closed away in the spare room and he didn't appear at all for the duration of my visit, but there wasn't a moment throughout that day that we weren't aware of him.

Sometimes, on stage, not showing something can be more powerful than showing it. The idea that murder or torture is taking place behind a closed door is more disturbing than watching actors grapple with each other, ineffectually mimicking horrors. And so it was that day in Molly's house. She went up a few times to see Fergus; I could hear soft voices and then the sound of the solid bedroom door closing behind her before she reappeared, looking worried and upset, but she said nothing about him and I knew better than to ask. At one point I went upstairs to the bathroom and from behind the shut door of the spare room I could hear the sound of someone crying, although to say that doesn't begin to do justice to it. It was the most heartbreaking sound I think I've ever heard, such suffering there was in it, such terrible abandonment and grief.

Thereafter, I always associated the spare room with Fergus, and I didn't like it. It was as if his sorrow was so intense it had infiltrated the curtains and the carpets, the very walls, and could never be eradicated. No matter how softly pretty its furnishings it had for me always an air of melancholy; I even fancied it was always a couple of degrees cooler than the other rooms in the house at any given time. This was nonsense, of course, as was the image that I conceived of Fergus. I could never forget that terrible weeping I had heard, and he became in my mind some kind of monster of grief, the embodiment of human misery. 'Unhappy.' That was as much as Molly would say about him for a long time. *Poor Fergus, he's so unhappy.* She was vague about what was actually wrong with him, vaguer still about the cause of it. But one thing soon became apparent to me: Fergus was the most important person in her life. She had a deep, almost fierce attachment to him that has, if anything, grown stronger with the passing of time.

The passing of time . . . the clock at the head of the

stairs chimed for noon. My computer screen had gone dark again, and with a mixture of resignation and relief I decided to give up for the day.

There were a few things I needed to buy before lunch – milk, bread, the newspapers – but I'd have gone out anyway, just to get away from the house, to distance myself from the dead end that had been the morning's work. I felt better as soon as the door closed behind me, and I stood there on the step for a moment, taking consolation from the glory of Molly's garden, its roses, its dog-daisies. The bright fresh morning had developed into a seriously hot day. As I closed the garden gate behind me, I thought of Andrew. A hot day in the city always made me think of his last days in Dublin, now so many years ago, when there had been weather such as this.

Andrew graduated from Trinity with a first-class honours degree, with prizes and a scholarship, in the same summer that I received the 2:2 that was far more than I deserved. Almost immediately he took himself off to England, to begin a PhD on Mantegna, at Cambridge. At that time I was living in a little redbrick terraced house in Dublin that was a smaller, more dowdy version of Molly's current home, and he stayed there with me just before he left Ireland. The two friends with whom I was sharing were both away for the week, and in the casual manner in which we then lived, I gave him his choice of the other girls' rooms for the two nights that he would be there. He arrived down from Belfast where he had been staying with his family, and I cautiously asked how things had been.

'We sat there last night,' he answered 'and I was trawl-

64

ing my brain for something to say to them, to ask them, and I couldn't think of a thing. There was nothing there. And I thought – who are these people? What am I doing here? I felt like a stranger who'd wandered in off the street and they'd decided to humour him and let him stay instead of throwing him out. And then when I was leaving this afternoon my Da came over all portentous, which was weird; I hadn't expected that. He said to me, "Try to make something of yourself, for Billy's sake." I thought, What's Billy got to do with it? Billy was never going to amount to anything; his life had been ruined when he was still a kid. He was always going to end up in jail or dead. I thought, I'm out of here, it's over.'

'And were your parents not pleased about your results?'

'My Da doesn't understand what it means, still doesn't know what I'm about. As for Ma, I just don't think she's ever really been interested in me. Billy was always the one she wanted, even when we were very small. He was always the joker, the funny one. I was too serious and dull, sitting with my nose in a book, while he'd be doing silly things and making her laugh. Because I knew she preferred him by far, that made me surly and then there was even less to like. I think she can't forgive me for not being Billy, or rather, she can't forgive me for being alive, and Billy being dead. He's still the one she wants, not me. When the train was going through Drogheda I looked down at the river, the timber yards, and I thought – if I never went back, never phoned, never wrote, would she care? Would she even notice?'

'You know she would,' I protested, to which Andrew gave a sardonic laugh. As at the time of Billy's death, I was struck by how he was more angry than grieved by the situation. Even that anger had dwindled with the passing of time; what he showed now was something closer to impatience and irritation.

All of this blighted the rest of that evening; but we didn't let it spoil the following day. The hot weather that tormented us all through our finals had, against our expectations, lingered on into the holidays, and Andrew's last day was glorious, perfect, a day such as today. We rose late and had breakfast in the overgrown, daisy-studded back garden, lingered until noon over peaches and orange juice and a few flabby croissants from the shop around the corner. It was unusual for Andrew not to have an exam for which to prepare, a seminar paper or an essay to write; and he was the better for it. The incredible pressure under which he'd put himself for the past four years had made him habitually edgy and tense, and it was good to see him begin to relax. Because his results had been so outstanding, he wouldn't have to prove himself to anybody when he went to Cambridge, he told me, 'Least of all to myself.' He was looking forward to being there and was excited about his new area of study.

I think one of the reasons I always look back on that day with such fondness is that it was a day lived between two lives, and therefore it managed to slip through the constraints of time itself. We were young, we were confident, we were hugely, even arrogantly, ambitious. Andrew was going to become an internationally acclaimed art historian, I was going to be a renowned playwright, and that we later succeeded in all of this only makes the memory of that day and its simple pleasures all the sweeter.

In the afternoon we went swimming at Seapoint. In honour of the fine weather my housemates and I had clubbed together to buy a barbecue. Andrew thought this was hilariously at odds with the lax and slipshod fashion in which we generally ran our shabby home, but that evening I badgered him into helping me light it. He seemed willing enough, and we incinerated a few chops and sausages, ate them with salad and bread and cheap red wine; then sat outside drinking and talking and laughing until long after a radiant summer darkness had fallen over the city.

He left for England early the following morning, and I never saw him again. That is to say, the Andrew whom I met in a Victorian pub in London at the end of that year wasn't the Andrew whom I had known at college. He had disappeared, taking with him his trainers, his rank jumpers and his sports bag full of books; and in his place was the dandified scholar who has been my friend ever since. Certainly there would be further fine tuning of the image over the years – the clothes would become more elegant and well-cut, the attention to detail would become total – but broadly speaking, the whole persona was already in place.

'It's great to see you again. What would you like to drink?' The Belfast accent had gone, and the pace and modulation of his voice had also changed. I watched him as he went up to the bar to order. He struck me as nervous, as well he might be, for he knew me to be both tactless and capable of cruelty. *Christ, what happened to you?* Carefully carrying two glasses, he made his way back through the crowds of drinkers to where I was sitting beneath an etched window of frosted glass, *wines &*

spirits. 'I've never seen you looking so well. England obviously suits you.'

'Thanks,' he replied. 'It does.' He relaxed a bit and started to tell me about how much he was enjoying his new life; that he had been down to Hampton Court recently to examine the *Triumphs of Caesar*, and was planning a trip to Italy. I had no sense of him pretending to be something he wasn't. There was nothing fake about him, nothing false. It was instead as if he was at last becoming himself, becoming the kind of person he needed to be, the person he really was. It was the tense, prickly man I'd known at college who had been the fake. I'd always been aware that he hadn't enjoyed his time as an undergraduate. How could he have done so? He hadn't been studying so much as trying to save his own life, and to expect him to be having a good time would have been as strange and heartless as calling out to a drowning man as he struggled to the shore, asking him if he was enjoying the swim.

In remembering all of this I had made my way to the shop, through the labyrinth of little streets of redbrick houses. Some of these houses, like Molly's, were well maintained, but others were dowdy and neglected, with net curtains drooping at dusty windows and front gardens strewn with rubbish. The shop itself was dispiriting too, like all convenience stores, as if one had to be punished simply for being there, for not being well enough organised to have got one's shopping elsewhere in the first place. Battered and fried things being kept warm under glass, tinned pies – how far gone did you have to be to eat a tinned pie? – exhausted fruit and a cart-load of lurid magazines. Molly has never been recognised here, not once, she told me proudly. She was just another local who had run out of coffee, sloping in mid-morning in a grey marl tracksuit and no make-up. I walked to the back of the shop. The milk was kept there, no doubt in the hope that customers might be tempted by something they saw on the way to the chill cabinet, a tin of strawberries, perhaps, or even one of those pies. I chose a loaf, then two newspapers from the stacks on the floor, paid at the till and left.

As I walked back I remembered again that I had had a wonderful dream just before waking that morning, but still I couldn't recall what it had been about. Only the atmosphere of it remained. The house itself seemed unnaturally dark after the brightness of the day, and was pleasantly cool. I dropped my shopping on the kitchen table. Lunch would be simple: bread, ham, fruit, coffee; I couldn't be bothered to prepare anything more elaborate. The table was a solid affair, large, rectangular, the wood scrubbed almost white.

The first time she raised the subject of birthdays, we'd been sitting here. I'd known Molly for about a couple of years by then. The subject must never have come up before, or if it did, she must have skilfully dismissed it, with so little ceremony that it didn't register with me. I saw her do this later with other people when I knew the significance of the subject to her, and although I was sympathetic – hugely sympathetic – to her position, I always found it slightly chilling to see the ease with which she could manipulate the direction of a conversation. *'Birthday? What do you want to know about my birthday for? Birthdays are for little children. Is it jelly you're after? Jelly and cake? Oh that reminds me, tell me now before I forget . . .'* And a new subject would be introduced; there would be no getting back to birthdays. There was nothing dishonest in it, yet still it felt like watching someone tell lies.

I was staying with her at the time. We'd been out, to dinner or to the cinema, I can't recall which, but when we came back it wasn't very late, probably no more than ten-thirty. There was an open bottle of red wine on the kitchen table. She offered me a glass and for the next hour or so we sat there talking and drinking. We were contented and relaxed and were still sitting there when the grandfather clock began to strike midnight. A silence fell over us. Inwardly I counted the chimes and after the last one I said, 'Today's the summer solstice. The longest day of the year,' to which Molly replied, 'It's my birthday today.'

'Happy birthday,' I said, and she gave a dry ironic laugh. 'Thanks.'

'Any plans for the day?'

'No.'

When you're in a hole, keep digging. 'Why don't you celebrate?' I mustn't have known her as well as I thought; now I would never be so foolish as to do such a thing. Now I know that Molly will never talk about anything significant at a time and a place where there is leisure and peace. Her most intimate and significant confidences will always be communicated in an off-the-cuff way, thrown over her shoulder as she goes out the door, as she jumps into a taxi. She didn't bridle or become annoyed at my question, but she didn't answer me either. I didn't break the silence that followed, and it became a long silence. I left it to her to take control of the conversation and change the subject, as I was sure she would.

She drank from her glass and then she said, 'I remember when I was about twelve. We lived in Lucan then. It was a difficult time. Fergus was more trouble than a bag of monkeys; my poor father was at his wits' end with him. Fainting fits, sleepwalking; he'd be poleaxed by pains that never seemed to have any real cause. So gentle he was too, though, Fergus, so sweet-natured.' She moved the foot of her glass across the table. By now it was almost as if she was talking to herself. 'I was always far more streetwise; I was a tough little madam. I looked after him; I fought his corner. And then when I hit puberty I fell apart too, but in a completely different way.

'I felt destroyed. It was as if I'd lost my soul. Up until then I'd been pretty well behaved, but practically overnight I became a delinquent. I started going about with this bunch of wild kids that I didn't even like. I'd cut class and take the bus into Dublin, go shoplifting. I stole things to order for my new friends. The things I stole for myself, sweets, make-up, little bits of jewellery, most of the time I didn't even want them, I'd end up throwing them away. I started drinking, I stayed out half the night, and when I was at home it was war. And through all of this, there was a voice, screaming and screaming inside my head. *Who am I? Who am I?* I thought I was going mad. Perhaps I was; I'd certainly lost my reason. All the bad behaviour was a way to try to drown out this terrible scream, *Who am I?* But nothing worked.

'And then the miracle happened. On one of the rare days that I did show up at school, they took us out to the theatre, to see *Hamlet*. I think it must have been a good production even though I had no point of comparison. They caught Hamlet's youth, that ironic anger he has, his

71

rage against his mother. Sneering when he wasn't in despair: that was me too. I'd never before seen anything so *real*. All of my life, and the past year in particular, was like a dream, and what I was watching on the stage, that was reality, that was the truth. In the interval I put my hand in my pocket and found a lipstick I'd stolen the day before. I remember staring at it, this little gilded cylinder. It was a thing from another life, the life that ended when I walked into the theatre. And as I watched the play through to the end I gradually came to realise something: *So that's who I am: I'm an actor*. This is a crucial distinction – it wasn't that I wanted to *be* an actor, I knew that I was one already. And it wasn't that I wanted to pretend to be other people either. All I ever wanted was to be myself. *Who am I? Who am I?* I never again heard that voice screaming in my head. I now knew exactly who I was. I was an actor. As soon as I was old enough I would go on stage and I would become other people. That was how I would spend the rest of my life.'

Perhaps unwittingly, she had just explained to me something important about her gift. Many actors spend years doing exactly what Molly had dismissed: they pretend to be other people. They select voices and movements that might plausibly suit a particular character, and they assume these voices and movements in the same way as they might put on a costume, a wig or a cardboard crown. It isn't convincing. Molly had understood this from the start. There was always something unmediated and supremely natural about her acting, it was the thing itself. Becoming, not pretending. It was a showing forth of her own soul, something about which she had always been fearless.

'So that's my life,' she said, and she turned and gave me a look, just as she spoke, which it wasn't, of course, it wasn't her whole life. What she had said begged more questions than it answered. But such a look! In it was all the pain of which she had spoken but which her voice had withheld, for she had spoken to me in neutral tones. There was anger, there was fear, bewilderment, and a passionate desire, a rage for love that could never be fulfilled. It was all there, a whole magma of dark emotion that could have destroyed her but which she had controlled and made central to her art. But still I didn't know what had caused this suffering, where it all came from. It would be quite some time before I found out. Molly looked away and the moment was gone.

'Let's finish this bottle out, and then I'll open another.' She topped up our glasses.

'This is enough for me,' I said, 'I'm fine.'

'Well I'm not.' She selected a new bottle from a small rack on the worktop and deftly removed the cork. The kitchen was dim, low-lit, and now she was alert as a cat, silent and tense. She emptied her glass and poured more wine. We couldn't find our way back into the conversation after what had passed between us, and eventually she suggested that I go up to bed if I wished. I left her there, for I sensed that she wanted to be alone. I lay awake for hours, and the clock had struck three before I heard the sound of her bedroom door closing.

I took my lunch and the newspapers out to the back garden, where I was joined by a neighbour's cat, a neat, greedy, ill-mannered creature that stuck its face in the milk jug and tried to get at the ham, until I had to move the tray well out of its reach. I read the colour supplement because it was easier to manage than the broadsheet; and in the list of contents I noticed a familiar name.

Reasons to be Cheerful is one of those features in which people with a new book, film, play or suchlike to promote do so by discussing the contents of their fridge or their handbag, showing off the finest room in their house or, as here, sharing with the public a list of things that make them happy. Most of the double spread on pages eight and nine was taken up with a striking photograph of Andrew, the text occupying a rather narrow column on the left-hand side. Several of his choices I could have second-guessed. Correggio, for example, at number two: *Quite simply my favourite painter*; or Chartres Cathedral at number seven. Several were as bland and anodyne as the concept of the piece implicitly required: *Dark chocolate, at least 70 per cent cocoa and Valhrona for choice*; but some were surprisingly robust: *Atheism. I detest religion. It has done untold harm and nothing would give me greater cause for celebration than if it were to die out completely.* There was no mention of his son, Anthony, which told me he was taking the whole thing in the spirit I would have expected – some things are too deep, too private to be referred to in so light a context. But listed there at number nine, between Venice and Beethoven's Grosse Fuge, was *The incomparable Molly Fox, our finest actress, bar none*. I wondered how she might react to this, whether the faux pas of the noun would cancel out the splendour of the adjective. At the bottom of the page was printed in italics: *Andrew Forde's new book, 'Remember Me: The Art of the Memorial' is published by Phaidon, price £30.00. The four-part documentary of the same name continues on Channel Four this evening at 8 p.m.*

The photograph had been taken in a room with the air of a gentleman's club. Andrew sat in a deep leather armchair, and on the wall behind him hung a gilt-framed painting of a winter landscape. He was wearing a pale blue shirt, open at the neck, and a dark blue jacket. Although he was sitting in a slightly unnatural pose, with all his fingers balanced delicately against each other at the tips, he looked relaxed and at ease, as he always does in any context connected with his work.

I think that Molly very much regrets that she didn't know Andrew before his great transformation. They didn't meet until about eight years ago, which was already about ten years after Andrew and I had left college. There were many logical and valid reasons as to why this should have been. During those first ten years when we were all in our twenties and busy consolidating our careers and our lives in general, there were long stretches when I saw little of either of them myself. Work commitments and other relationships, friends and family, kept us occupied and apart. When Andrew got married I didn't much care for his wife, Nicole, nor she for me, and we perhaps saw less of each other because of that.

But I would be lying if I didn't admit that the main reason they never met was that I deliberately kept them apart for years on end, and for the best possible reason – I thought they wouldn't like each other. Andrew knew and admired Molly as an actor and had even begun to pester me a bit about her. *When are you going to introduce me to that amazing friend of yours?* I knew that this was exactly the wrong approach to take with her. One of the strange anomalies of Molly is that she has never, I think, successfully developed a public persona in which to conceal and protect herself in society; another harder, somewhat untrue personality that can be passed off as the real thing. She always was, and remains, painfully shy. Quite frankly, I feared that Andrew would find her a disappointment, mousy and introverted, dull even, so unlike the magisterial presence he knew from the stage. I had seen this happen before, and Molly did nothing to prevent it. In social situations she might well be deliberately taciturn and sullen. And if I thought Andrew might not get along with Molly, I was completely certain that she would dislike him. She is a merciless student of human nature, and while she finds her greatest truth in life through the artifice that is her gift, I thought that in the artifice that was Andrew she would find nothing but pure surface, and despise him.

My own birthday is around the end of the year, and eight years ago I decided to throw a combined Christmas and birthday party at my home in London. By this time Molly, like half the country, had become familiar with Andrew through his career as a television art critic, and she had begun to ask to meet him, as he asked to meet her. It seemed the best idea to invite them both to the party. If they got on together, well and good; if not, there would be enough people there for them to simply withdraw and talk to someone else. I had little time to speak to either of them that evening. As the giver of the party, I was too busy making sure that everyone had something to eat and drink, that no one was excluded or ill at ease. I did notice that Molly and Andrew were talking, but not monopolising each other. When I spoke to them in the following days I was slightly surprised by their reactions. I got the impression that Andrew had found her slightly intimidating, a reaction she rarely elicits, and while she had clearly enjoyed his company, what interested her most about him was precisely that change in him that I had spoken about and which she had not witnessed for herself.

'He's a study. That accent! Where did that come from, those vowel combinations? I've never heard the like of it. And did you notice his cufflinks? Little bars of lapiz lazuli.' Yes, I had noticed the cufflinks. Molly is not the only one whose profession has sharpened her eye for detail, but I was surprised at how much she picked up on the speech, because Andrew's accent is most convincing. 'What on earth was he like when you knew him first?' She was very curious about this, and quizzed me about exactly how he had changed. At the time I put this down to the actor's interest in the transformation of the self. Now I'm not so sure. I think she found my answers unsatisfactory, and I grew to resent having to try to explain it. In some ways he had changed completely, in others not at all. The way he looked, the way he dressed and spoke, yes, all that had changed comprehensively. In another man these changes might have made him seem effete and affected, but in Andrew they simply seemed right. There was a robust quality to both his mind and his personality that remained constant, that complemented his new manners and suited them perfectly. His essential self, in as far as I could understand it, hadn't changed at all.

But Molly couldn't get it. 'So it's purely a surface thing then?'

'No. He was angry when I knew him first and that's gone. He's much less sardonic. He's become the person he needed to be, and he's been able to relax into that.'

'Have you slept with him?'

'Molly! What a question!'

'I take it that's a *Yes*?' she said coolly.

'It's a *No*. It's an *Absolutely not*.'

I could hardly believe her cheek. Although we were close we were both quite reserved with each other. I think a certain kind of mutual respect was one of the reasons as to why our friendship was so strong. Of course we confided in each other about many things, but we never fished for information, never followed up casual signals or leads. If there was something one of us wanted to share with the other, she would tell it in her own time. I knew that she might sometimes ask someone a staggeringly frank and direct question, but she always did it as a tactic, as a way of wrong-footing the other person, distracting them when they were perhaps getting too close to something that she didn't want to reveal. It was a way of throwing people off balance. She had never before done it to me.

Obviously our friendship would survive such a thing; her friendship with Andrew was another story. If it had been down to me they would never have met again, a rather small-minded, even spiteful reaction I admit. I would certainly never have brought them into each other's company; but some months after their first meeting at my house, they bumped into each other by chance. It was late at night in the centre of London. Andrew was on his way home from a concert, and Molly had just left the theatre where she had been performing. They went off together for a drink, Andrew told me, and sat talking for hours. It was on that night, rather than at my party, that their friendship had really begun.

It was something of a relief to me to learn all this. I had realised by then that I'd over-reacted to Molly's remark, and that if she and Andrew got on well together then for all three of us to be friends made perfect sense. Together we were more than the sum of our parts. They were my oldest, my closest friends, and what developed between us was an enrichment of what was already there, what I already had with each of them separately. And it gave me pleasure to watch these two people, who I knew so well and of whom I was so fond, gradually get to know each other. It gave me pleasure to watch the friendship of my two best friends grow and develop.

On occasion Molly would ask me leading questions about him, but I wouldn't be drawn; I didn't feel it was appropriate. It was up to Andrew himself to tell her about his life and in due course he did: about how he had met his wife Nicole while they were both postgraduate students in Cambridge. They had married as soon as their studies were completed and moved to London, where she took up a job with an auction house and he began working at the Courtauld Institute. Their son Tony was born four years later, and by the time he was five the marriage was over. Molly was made aware of these bald facts but was left to divine for herself their true emotional weight and significance. You have to think of Oscar and Bosie to envisage the degree of *amour fou* of which Andrew is capable. *How could I not love him? He ruined my life.* Does Molly know even yet, I wonder, that Andrew's loves have about them the quality of obsession? I remember this from the time we were at university together and he fell for a classmate, who was also a friend of mine, with such a degree of passion and intensity that I, callow girl that I then was, couldn't quite comprehend it.

Her name was Marian Dunne. She was a vet's daughter from County Kildare and she was studying History of Art and French. 'There's Andrew Forde. He asked me to go to Trinity Ball,' she said to me one afternoon as he sloped past at a distance, unaware that we were watching him. 'Just imagine!'

'He's a really decent guy,' I said, and she agreed, with mild regret. She was gentle in manner, pretty, with long fair hair that she wore swept up into a complicated arrangement, secured with lacquered clips. Marian was decent too. She was sensible to the good heart concealed beneath the rancid jumper, but couldn't quite bring herself to get beyond the fact of the jumper. Suddenly even I could see that Andrew as he then was, scruffy, broke and blunt of manner, hadn't a hope. This made me say, perversely, 'You should go to the ball with him.' Marian didn't reply. We watched him walk out of our line of vision and then she sighed. 'It's a pity,' she said, and it was.

But it was only when she started going out with a fourth-year medical student and it developed into a steady relationship that I began to understand how deeply affected Andrew was. Rejection only made the attachment stronger. I realised that the impossibility of connection was a driving force behind his desire. This made me lose patience with him. He wanted Marian precisely because he couldn't have her; and it was aspirational too, I thought: he was the snob in wanting her, not she in turning him down. I put it down to too much time spent on art, too much time spent gazing at paintings of saints and goddesses, perfected, unattainable, impossible women. I took to creeping up to him at his library desk and whispering in his ear, 'You should get out more.' He never spoke to me about his feelings, but I was aware of them all the same, as on the day when I finally had to tell him, 'Marian's going to an engagement party tonight.'

'Whose?' he said.

'Her own.'

'Oh,' he said, and it was a small cry, but full of pain, as if he'd been burnt or stung.

With Nicole it was different. Perhaps because his love was reciprocated, or because his own life had changed by then, he had the confidence to declare himself freely. 'I just adore her,' he said, the first time he told me about Nicole. Not long before they left Cambridge for London I visited them at the house they shared, where already the rooms were full of tea chests and packing cases. Nicole was a silent, smiling woman. The big room was flooded in light, and she sat on a broad windowsill, at a slight distance from us. Andrew was in high good humour about the move. 'We've been really fortunate, someone we know here owns a flat in Highgate that's just fallen vacant, so we'll be renting that in the first instance. It's a beautiful place, isn't it?' Nicole smiled and nodded. She was dressed in cream; she looked cool in spite of the heat of the day. You could spend a lifetime, I thought, looking at that lovely face and wondering at the nuances of its speechless expression: affection, condescension, contempt. Nicole was like a force of nature, like a cosmic void into which energy vanished. I saw that she could absorb anger as easily as adoration and still keep smiling calmly. She said nothing against me, was in no way hostile, and yet I realised as I walked away from the house afterwards that not since my final afternoon in Lucy's employ had I felt myself to be so comprehensively dismissed. And in spite of all this I believed that Andrew could be happy with her, because, as Molly says, we all do get what we really want in life. We make a point of it, although sometimes we choose not to own it. Andrew wanted to be the adorer, not the adored; in any relationship he wanted to worship. Sometimes what we want is not in our own best interests. Sometimes we hunger for our own destruction. *How could I not love him? He ruined my life.*

By now the cat that had been trying to pilfer my lunch was sitting on top of the fibreglass cow. It looked funny, as they were both black and white but one was so tiny and active, the other immense and inert. The cat was sitting on the cow's head. It patted the point of one of the cow's horns with its paw, as though testing for sharpness. Then it turned around with amazing dexterity and walked away. It sat down on the cow's wide back and gazed up at the sun. With slow deliberation the cat began to wash its face.

I looked again at the photograph in the magazine, at the dim splendour of the room, at Andrew's face. Was I disappointed that he hadn't been able to find a place for me in his list, that he hadn't called me *incomparable, our finest playwright bar none*? Perhaps. I thought that maybe he put me in the same category as his son Tony; that our relationship was too special to be vulgarised in this way. I have known Andrew for longer than anyone else in his life, of that I'm certain. By the time he and Molly met they were both successful and established, there's no comparison. I remembered that last day Andrew and I spent in Dublin, now more than twenty years ago, the light on the sea, how the blue night fell.

I put the magazine aside and took up the newspaper. There was a surprise there too, as I leafed through it. Tucked in under the obituaries was a small column devoted to recording the birthdays of famous people that fell on that day. There, in amongst the high court judges and the cricketers, the senior civil servants and the celebrity chefs, was *Molly Fox, actress, 40.*

Molly would go wild when she found out about this. It was just as well she was out of the country. How had this come about? And was it even true? Was she really forty today? Strange as it may seem, I didn't know. I thought she would have turned forty two years earlier. I would pass that particular milestone myself at the end of this year, and I had always been under the impression that she was a couple of years older than me.

There were two reasons as to why I wasn't sure. Firstly, there was her general distaste for birthdays. Because of what had happened in the past she never celebrated on this day. I knew better than to offer presents or a cake, it would only have annoyed her. I remember one year being with her on the twenty-first of June as she opened her post, and in amongst the bills and circulars was a card. Whether it was from a close friend or a theatre-goer I have no idea, but she glanced at its gaudy motif of candles and balloons, rolled her eyes in exasperation, and then threw the card in the bin without further comment. That was Molly's attitude to her birthday.

Her attitude to her age was more typical. Like a great many women actors she was deliberately vague about how old she was for a good reason: she was afraid of being passed over for roles. 'If people know you're thirty they won't cast you as a twenty-five-year-old no matter how young you look,' she had remarked to me once. The much older actor who had played the mother in *The Yellow Roses* had expressed it to me with far more bitterness, staring at her own wrinkled, unmade-up face in the harshly lit mirror of her dressing room: 'There's no profession that despises older women more than the theatre does.' Duplicity about one's age was therefore understandable, indeed it was downright common sense. But was Molly really forty today? I had no idea.

I would buy her a present for all that, or perhaps a series of small presents, which I knew she preferred, as tokens to thank her for the loan of the house. I would get her a book and some hand-made chocolates, what else, I didn't know. I carried the tray with the ruins of lunch back into the house, but as I was clearing up at the sink, I broke Molly's milk jug. I swore violently at myself for my own clumsiness even as the jug was exploding on the quarry tiles in a mess of milk and bits of ceramic. I would replace it when I was in town that afternoon I told myself as I picked up the biggest pieces and put them in the bin, and wondered where the mop was kept. That is, I would buy her another jug, but the piece I had broken was really irreplaceable. Like most of her possessions it was particular and unusual. It had a matching sugar bowl and she had told me once, when I admired them, that they had been bought in Russia. Blue and white they were, the blue intense as lapis, and handsomely set off by the white motif, by the fine gold line around the rim. And now I had broken the jug and ruined the set.

Oddly enough, I knew that Molly wouldn't mind. I knew exactly what she would say: *These things mean nothing.* I was often surprised by the contexts in which she used this phrase. She'd said it when she herself cracked a glass vase of which I knew she was particularly fond, by rinsing it under a cold tap immediately after having washed it in scalding water. Her annoyance lasted for seconds, and then it was over, dismissed with precisely those words with which I knew she would dismiss the fate of the milk jug. I have always found it hard to square her acquisitive nature, her fondness for things, with her complete non-attachment to them. She would show these objects to me, these tokens and trinkets, with a childlike simplicity of heart: a wooden candlestick, an enamelled box, a fragment of antique lace. And then one day she handed me a small bowl made of olive-wood and she said to me shyly, 'Tom gave me this.'

Tom. My Tom. They met for the first time during the first run of *Summer with Lucy* but only really got to know each other a couple of years later, by which time I was settled in London. By then the discrepancy between my life as a playwright and my other life as a member of my family bothered me greatly. One way of dealing with it was to keep them strictly separate, and in many ways this was easy. The geographic distance helped. Then my parents and siblings, while displaying a pleasing pride in me and enthusiasm for my progress, my successes, also had a useful lack of curiosity about what it was that I was actually about. Although they sent me cards and phoned to wish me luck, to congratulate me on any new production, they rarely came to see the work, and when they did, had no problem in cheerfully declaring themselves bamboozled. And this suited me fine.

The problem was Tom. Tom was the link between my two worlds. It was, after all, he who had introduced me to the theatre in the first place, and so it seemed churlish now to exclude him from it. But I was trying to protect him, I told myself. I had come a long way from when I was Lucy's cleaner and would no longer artlessly announce to all comers that my brother was a Catholic priest. It only took a couple of unkind remarks to teach me to keep such information to myself. Tom's idea of a good time was to come to visit me in London for a few days. He would trawl the book and music shops during the day, look at paintings, and then in the evening meet up with me and we would go to see a play. That was what he suggested to me for his first visit over. It sounded fine by me, and it set the pattern for many visits to come.

I went out to meet him at Heathrow, but when he arrived my delight at seeing him was tempered with dismay: he was in full clerical garb. Why did this surprise me? The dark clothes and dog collar were such a part of him that it shouldn't have done so. Suddenly it struck me that I wouldn't just be going round London for the next few days with my brother Tom, I'd be going round London with a priest. On the Tube in from the airport I wondered if I could ask him to tone it down a bit: a grey, open necked shirt and a black suit would be enough. But I hadn't the heart. I didn't want to hurt him and I said nothing.

I'm ashamed to admit that I didn't feel wholly comfortable with him for the duration of that first visit. I kept him strictly to myself, I didn't introduce him to any of my friends. It disturbed me to see him out of context, and I hadn't expected this at all. I was aware of things I hadn't noticed before, and I found it hard to realise that I didn't really know him as well as I had thought. He struck me as very much the country priest, the farmer's son, and his accent was stronger and more marked than I'd realised until now. Tom, thank goodness, gave absolutely no indication that he knew what was going through my mind. I think he was far too busy enjoying himself.

I settled down in England in the following years, and Tom made at the very least an annual visit to me. As I became more secure in my new life I began to recognise the snobbery there was in my attitude to my brother, and I hated myself for it. The next time he was over I resolved to introduce him to some of my friends and colleagues. Even though I was involved with Ken by that time – it was about a year since we'd all worked together, me and Molly and David and Ken – I excluded him from any possible meeting. At the time I could hardly have said why. It was something I didn't even want to think about and, with hindsight, it had more to do with deep-seated reservations about Ken rather than any problem with Tom. There was always Molly, of course. She was in London at that time, in rehearsal for the role of the daughter in *The Glass Menagerie*, and when I suggested to her that the three of us meet one evening for dinner, she readily accepted.

She arrived late to the restaurant, apologetic and somewhat flustered. I could see at once that something was up. Part of the problem was, I think, her shyness, something I still found hard to square with the very public nature of her work, although I have since come to accept that the two are not mutually exclusive. She was that evening, at least to begin with, in her closed mode, and came across as mousy, dowdy. Tom, on the other hand, energised by the city, showed forth all his intelligence and good nature. The contrast between them was striking. There was something I noticed about Tom on this visit that I couldn't fathom: he kept reminding me of David McKenzie. The first time it struck me, I actually laughed out loud in surprise. *What is it?* Tom said. *Nothing. Nothing at all.* How could this be? My brother is stocky, jowly, with something of a paunch, so it wasn't a physical resemblance, that was for sure. It wasn't idiom of speech either, nor any particular mannerism. I watched Tom now as he talked to Molly, as he ordered from the waiter, hoping for a clue.

Molly then told us about a disagreement that she had had that afternoon with her director. 'He sat us all down and said, "Today I want to look at the mother in this play and I want you all to share with us something of how you feel about your own mother." Some directors seem to want to turn the whole rehearsal process into a big therapy session. And I realise some actors like that. They want to do a certain kind of research – if they're playing a homeless person they'll go out and spend a night on a park bench. I don't see the point in that, because even while you're lying on the bench you know that you have a nice safe bed at home and that you'll be in it the following night, so you aren't finding out at all what it's like to be homeless. My approach is more direct; I like to just think my way into a role. A lot of it's common sense and using your imagination. Of course you have to dig into your own emotions, your own feelings and experiences. I think some actors like to share all that with the company; it makes them feel closer to the people with whom they're going to work, whereas I think it should go straight into the work. It's down to me to translate my own experience into the role, and I tried to explain that to the director.' I knew the person in question.

'So you had an argument?' I said.

'We most certainly did.'

'I've often thought there are great similarities between being an actor and being a priest,' Tom remarked unexpectedly, 'although don't tell my bishop I said that.'

Molly laughed. 'No, seriously,' he said. 'There's obviously a certain theatrical side to what I do, in that you have to become at different times the person people need you to be at that particular moment. Which isn't to say that I'm insincere or pretending, any more than the theatre is about pretence. Well, it is at one level, but it isn't at all on another, if you see what I mean.' I did, but I was surprised, for what he said bespoke a deep understanding of acting, much deeper than I would have expected. 'It's my role in life, quite literally, and I'm seldom out of costume,' and he gestured to his collar. 'But it's always really me.'

'Then it's exactly the same as being an actor,' Molly said.

'Not exactly, but similar, yes. It's a way of translating your whole self.'

With that, the waiter brought our starters, and for a moment I thought that Molly was going to ask him to take them away again. She wanted to go on quizzing Tom, and the food had become an unwelcome distraction to her. Fortunately her line of questioning had caught his imagination. 'I suppose what's similar about being an actor and being a priest is a certain perception of time. Eternity is a priest's business. But we all live in time. And what I'm doing is trying to make people aware of how the two coexist. That's what religion is, keeping that sense of eternity while being in time; and trying to live accordingly. *The Kingdom of God is here, now*. That's what that's all about.'

'And what about the theatre then?'

Tom thought about this. 'What about the theatre? Well, it exists in time – a play lasts an hour and a half, two hours, but if it's any good at all it takes you somewhere outside time. And then you can see things – see things differently. But then, who am I to say that? You're the actor and you're the playwright. What do I know about the theatre?' He picked up the bread-basket and offered it to me. I had already started eating some moments earlier, but still Molly sat there and didn't lift her cutlery. She was staring at Tom. Sometimes Molly reminds me of a cat. She has that same stillness, that concentrated energy, that steady, unblinking gaze. Suddenly Tom put down his fork again.

'Last week, I called to visit a family in my parish. They have a lot of difficulties, a lot of social problems. The father drinks heavily and there's a strong sense of domestic violence, although the mother denies it. Social services are on the case and there are small children involved. It's all very sad. The father runs a breaker's yard from right beside the house. The place is surrounded by old broken rusty wrecks of cars; it's as bleak a spot as you can imagine. I parked and went up to the house, where one of the daughters of the family, Eileen, who's about five, was sitting on the doorstep crying. Her hair is badly cut, with a big square fringe that doesn't flatter her at all; and her face was blotched and red. I don't know when I last saw such a grimy, pitiful little scrap of humanity. I said hello and asked her how she was. She didn't reply and I hunkered down beside her. "Is something wrong? Do you want to tell me?" Still she said nothing, but she sniffed and shook her head. She was holding a Barbie-type doll, and even by Barbie standards it was quite over the top. It had a tiara and transparent wings, blonde hair and a gold dress covered in sequins. "Is that you?" I asked. She looked up at me and she smiled. "That's me," she said. "I'm really a princess."

"I could tell that," I said.

"I'm a princess and sometimes I'm a fairy, and I'm a mermaid too." I thought she was marvellous. She knew her own worth, she insisted on it. She knew that no matter how miserable the circumstances in which life placed her, she was better than that. She knew that a part of her was special and remarkable, and she was able to articulate that in her own way. "I'm a princess and sometimes I'm a fairy, and I'm a mermaid too.'"

'What made you mention that, just now?' Molly said.

'I'm not sure. Eileen, indeed her whole family, have been very much on my mind in the past few days. I wish I could do more to help them, change their circumstances in some way. Forgive me for talking shop, this is foolish of me. I'm distracting you from your dinner,' Tom said to Molly, and he gestured to her to eat. 'I hope I'm not annoying you, saying foolish things about your profession. It's only speculation on my part. Why don't you tell me what it's like being an actor.'

'I don't know – it's hard to say.' She was abstracted, and I could see that she had been thinking of something else entirely. 'There are two schools of thought on acting,' I said to help her out. 'Some people consider actors to be vain, silly people who only want to show off. And some think they're incredibly brave – not for the way they embrace a life with so much insecurity and rejection hardwired into it, but for the way they put their whole self out there.'

'There are as many ways of being an actor as there are people who act,' Molly said. 'That's the beauty of it, that it's so individual. Some are quite restrained and understated, some completely manic.'

'Surely that depends on the role?'

'Not in the way I'm thinking. It's always about energy, energy either released and displayed, or held back and controlled; but one way or another it has to be there. If it isn't, you're just seeing bad acting. Some actors, like me, are chameleons, they transform themselves completely. And then there are other actors who are always just themselves. That isn't to say that they're bad at what they do; that they can't act. Some of the finest actors who have ever worked in the theatre are like this. What I mean is that they have a highly developed persona in their everyday life that closely resembles what they present in their work. The public accepts it perhaps without fully understanding it or being aware of it, so deep is the convention. You tend to see it more in the cinema than on stage, and to be honest you don't see it that often. The more protean type, the kind of thing I do, is more usual. Take David now, for example,' she said, turning to me. 'David McKenzie. He's a classic example. He's a wonderful actor, but he's always himself.'

It startled me that she should so suddenly mention him, when I'd been thinking intently about him in relation to Tom. It was almost as if she could read my mind, and it spooked me.

'Is he the actor who was in your last play?' Tom asked me, and I nodded.

'He's working on a film at the moment,' Molly said. 'He's going to be a huge star, wait and see. He's got everything going for him.'

By this stage she appeared to have relaxed into the situation. She ate her salad and chatted to Tom about the theatre, about the play he and I were to see later that evening. I withdrew somewhat from the conversation and studied my brother. Why had I been so worried about bringing him into my new life? It was more than just a social thing. Many of my friends were openly hostile to the church and with good reason. I fully understood their anger. I would probably have made much more of a distance from it myself had it not been for Tom, by which I don't mean mere family loyalty. Even if he hadn't been my brother he'd have given me pause for thought, had he crossed my path. The very least he could do was make you consider the possibility of the divine in a world where the notion was generally scorned. I had often wondered how someone as mentally sophisticated as Tom endured his life. He was at that time a curate in the small mid-Ulster town where one of our sisters lived with her family. I had met his parish priest, with whom he shared a house: a humourless and unimaginative man who went through the rituals of his vocation, conducting marriages and funerals, saying Mass, as if it were all meaningless and functional. Tom has an exceptionally good mind. All through my teens it was he who had fed my imagination, been my intellectual mentor and companion. He'd introduced me not only to the theatre, but to Russian literature and Baroque music. He countered the pietistic Catholicism to which I was exposed at home and at school, all medals and miracles, by giving me books by St John of the Cross and St Teresa of Avila; he told me about Charles de Foucauld and about Liberation theology. And I took it all for granted. I didn't realise that he was setting my mind free, that he was giving me a life. Nor did I realise how much I meant to him. Sitting in that London restaurant I remembered being home for a weekend during my first year at university and suddenly Tom had blurted out to me when there was no one else around: 'I miss you.' At the time I didn't understand. It was only now I realised how lonely he must have been after I'd gone.

The rest of the meal passed over pleasantly enough, as far as I can recall. Nothing of any great consequence was said, and my memory of it has been somewhat eclipsed by what happened afterwards on the Tube. The three of us set out together although Molly, who was going home, was to get out at the stop before us to change lines. In the train we managed to secure for ourselves seats for four, two and two facing. I sat beside Molly, and Tom was facing us. I think the rolling stock must have been very old, because it was particularly noisy; we could barely hear each other. We had, I thought, by that stage fallen into the platitudes and courtesies with which one wraps up such an evening, when there is little time left for anything real to be said. 'It was lovely to meet you at last, having heard so much about you,' Molly shouted at Tom. 'You're fortunate to have each other, to come from such a happy family. When I think about my own childhood . . . My mother walked out on my brother and me when I was seven.' So extraordinary was this information to me, so offhand the delivery and so strange the circumstances in which she had chosen to share it, that for a moment I thought I must have surely misheard. I glanced over at Tom, but his face was quite impassive.

The train pulled out of the tunnel and into the brightness of the station at Piccadilly Circus. Molly stood up. 'I hope we meet again before long,' she said, leaning over and pressing her hand on Tom's forearm. Her voice, which had been forced and harsh as she shouted out the great secret of her life, reverted now to its usual sweetness. 'I'll phone you during the week,' she said as she turned to me. 'Enjoy the play,' and again to Tom in particular, 'All the best for the rest of your time in London.' Then she was gone, minding the gap, disappearing into the dense, swarming crowds on the platform. The doors slammed shut and the train moved on. Neither Tom nor I spoke. The appropriate conversation wouldn't have been possible over the racket, and when we arrived at our stop we hurried because we were late. At the theatre there was time to do nothing more than buy a programme and take our seats.

In spite of Molly's good wishes, I didn't enjoy the play. It was a contemporary work, one that has since been justly forgotten, and I don't know how it had garnered the good reviews that had lured Tom and me there. I spent the whole of the first half sitting in the darkness watching the actors rant and emote on the lit stage as I thought about what Molly had said just before we parted, trying to square it with what I already knew about her life.

Over the few years I had known her she had drip-fed me bits of information. A suburban childhood in a semi-detached house. A father who had worked at some kind of office job, who died just after she left school and of whom she always spoke warmly, whom she had evidently loved. A younger brother who was deeply troubled in himself (I had not yet met Fergus at this stage, but I had heard him weeping behind the closed door) and to whom she was fiercely loyal, viscerally close. A mother whom she almost never mentioned, and then always disparagingly. Once, for example, we had been out shopping together and had seen a particularly dreadful handbag. It had a large piece of crystal incorporated into the clasp, and was the kind of thing that could not be redeemed from vulgarity, not even by the most highly developed sense of irony or fondness for kitsch. 'My mother would love it,' Molly sneered. Another time she had mentioned something about the time her father passed away and I asked her if her mother was also dead. 'Oh no, she's still around, she's out there somewhere, living her life,' she replied, but it was the short, dry laugh that preceded this remark that said still more, that chilled me. What she had said this evening did fit the picture I had had: it all added up, it did make sense now.

I suppose I expected that Tom had been thinking along the same lines as me, but when the interval finally came and the lights went up he turned to me with a sigh and said, 'Oh well, some you win, some you lose.' We talked only about the play, and although he mentioned later how much he had liked meeting Molly he didn't pick my brains about her, as anyone else might have done. He did ask me very late one night, completely out of context,

'That thing Molly said to us about her mother – did you already know about that?'

'No,' I said, 'I didn't.'

'I see,' he replied, and he said nothing more.

The following week, after Tom had gone back to Ireland, Molly asked me for his address. She wanted, she said, to drop him a note, to say what a pleasure it had been to meet him. I thought she perhaps felt embarrassed at what she had said at the moment of parting. It wasn't mentioned again to me, and I knew not to refer to it. Molly sets the tone for any encounter: from day one I have always known instinctively what not to say, when she wanted an issue addressed, and when it was strictly off limits. I gave her the address and heard no more about it, from either Molly or Tom, indeed I thought no more about it until a year later, when my brother wasn't long back from a pilgrimage to Jerusalem and Molly showed me the little olive-wood bowl: 'Tom gave me this.'

I had had no idea they'd been in contact with each other all this time, and yet how could I not have seen it coming? I should have known on that day in London that already she had recognised him as someone whom she needed in her life, someone who could help her. No, I hadn't realised that it was happening, and I resented it when I found out. While Molly is undoubtedly generous with her possessions, she can take over other people's friendships and relationships as a cuckoo takes over nests. But what was it that really bothered me in all of this? Was it that I didn't want to share Tom with Molly or that I didn't want my brother too closely linked to my other life, my life away from the family? Probably both were an issue and yes, it does pain me to know how small-minded all of this shows me up to be. Tom is a good listener. He is compassionate and intelligent, with a rare degree of moral knowledge and experience.

Molly on the other hand was more deeply wounded, more damaged by her early years than I could then imagine. She is also ardently although not conventionally religious; and like much else in her life this is something that she conceals rather well. Her childhood introduction to religion was made in an uninspiring suburban church, a barn of a place, to which she and Fergus would be taken on Sunday mornings by her father. It had nothing of the mystery, the earthed connection to place, to the seasons, that I knew from my own childhood church in the country. For all that, something got through to Molly, some spark, something that she needed in her life and that she has quietly cherished ever since.

The gift of the wooden bowl happened many years ago, and now there are other little tokens of Tom's affection scattered around the house. An edition of the Psalms bound in dark green morocco. A rosary with pearl beads. A tiny Greek icon. I take for granted their friendship now, even though it remains something from which I am generally excluded.

Having finished with the lunch dishes, I decided to go into town and try to replace the jug I had broken. I stood in the hall for a moment to check that I had everything I needed – keys, money, basket, list. I also took a notebook with me in case I had a good idea about my work while I was out, unlikely though that was. I paused just before leaving. The hallway of Molly's house is arresting, because she has made of it a small shrine to her career, to her success. The walls are covered with framed posters of productions in which she has starred, together with striking black-and-white photographs: Molly as Ophelia, as Lady Macbeth, as Hedda Gabler. There is a chest of drawers the top of which is covered with awards she has won: great chunks of cut glass, gilded masks, semi-abstract figurines. I do not know how she lives with this, and I have told her so. My own awards – and there are a considerable number of them – are either in my family home or hidden away in cupboards and drawers. On a day such as today when I'm struggling with the work and failing to make any progress they would seem to me more like a mockery than a valediction. Molly and I were in her hall when we talked about this, and I could see that she was only half-listening, smiling up at these proofs of her triumph. 'Do you really think so?' she said. 'It always cheers me up to look at them. I wouldn't have it any other way.'

The early-afternoon sun was strong on the front of the house when I left. I stepped out into the heat, into a great sweetness, a complex of fragrances: cut grass from someone's lawn, and lavender, robust, overlain with the peculiarly fragile scent of sweet pea. As I walked away from the house I wondered at the facility some people have for creating a home for themselves. Molly can do it, Andrew too, but it has always eluded me. The places I have lived in have remained only that: places I have lived in; rooms full of papers and books. I should like a proper home not just for my own sake but because it would be an extension of me, and would allow me to communicate something of myself to others. But how people managed to do this with the things I glimpsed in the houses I passed –

candles, rugs, bentwood chairs, dressers and lamps – baffled and defeated me.

In a tiny basement area of one house an old man was sunning himself, surrounded by plants in containers. He was wearing braces over a striped shirt with the sleeves rolled up, and a white straw hat was tilted to conceal his eyes. Seeing him, I was suddenly reminded of my dream of the night before, not just the atmosphere but the substance of it. For the first time since waking that morning I remembered the dream precisely – my grandmother, the shoes, the blanket, the feeling of being loved and protected. And this in turn triggered another memory, something that I had forgotten for years, of a fruit shop in the south of France where the woman behind the counter was identical to my late grandmother, and so strong was the resemblance that I became convinced that it was indeed her. She didn't recognise or acknowledge me, but kept on weighing out the fruit for which I kept on asking. I bought cherries and apricots, grapes and plums, more than I wanted, more than I could ever possibly eat, simply to keep open the line of communication with her. *This is my grandmother*. Even as all of this was happening I knew that it was absurd. How could someone be dead and buried in Ireland and then be selling fruit in Provence years later? It wasn't just that she looked like my grandmother, she moved like her, had the same habit of smoothing down her apron; she emanated the same sweetness of nature. I stopped asking for fruit when my grandmother remarked as to whether or not I would be able to carry all I had.

All I could feel afterwards was gratitude that this had happened. Being able to understand it was of no great importance. We see no visions because we live in an age in which they are not permitted; but if we accepted the idea of them, who's to say what we wouldn't see? Marriage is no longer a mystical union but a social contract. The moment when new beliefs reach critical mass and become generally accepted always eludes us, we are always looking away. Thereafter I would think from time to time about whatever it was that had happened that day in the fruit shop; in due course I thought about it less and less. But it was doubtless the memory of that uncanny meeting, deep in my unconscious, that had triggered the dream of last night. And for that too I was grateful.

I passed a house where the front door lay open, and I could hear a woman's light voice deep within, at the end of the darkened hall. There were bunches of coloured balloons tied to the door knocker, more on the gate, and the garden fence was festooned with streamers and a foil banner: *Seven Today!* When Molly eventually told me that her mother had left not just in her seventh year, but on her seventh birthday, she did so in the laconic, off-hand way in which I had by now come to expect when she was telling me something important. *She knows how to pick her moment, my mother. You have to give her that, if nothing else.* I forced myself to think again about the play on which I was working, about the man with the hare, in the hope of breaking the impasse I had reached. I had very little to go on so far, scraps of ideas, a general intuition. I could hear a child's voice saying, *Nothing must change.* That phrase had been embedded in my mind almost as long as the image of the hare in the man's arms, and I knew they were linked, but I hadn't been able to find the vital connection and get on with the work.

I was walking in Molly's footsteps now, taking the particular route into town that she had pointed out to me as being the quickest and also the most interesting: the route where there was most to see. She had walked these streets by herself time without number, and I had walked them with her on many occasions. She had pointed out to me the things she liked along the way. The massive clump of arum lilies that crowded out all the space of a tiny garden. The white oblong stones at the top of certain houses, carved with pointing hands and the names of the streets. The little tree that brought forth a startling foam of blossom each springtime, a tree so small and insignificant that one never noticed it when its branches were bare; it always seemed, Molly said, to have appeared overnight. In recognising such things we claim the city, make it our own. *I never cross the Green that I don't think of Countess Markievicz; never am in Merrion Square that I don't think of Oscar.* Oscar the child, she meant, she said when I pressed her, the tall boy who played with his friends in the enclosed garden but who noticed and who never forgot the children of the Dublin paupers, glimpsed on the other side of the railings. *Every afternoon as they were coming from school, the children used to go and play in the Giant's garden.*

As I walked along the hot streets the houses gave way now to offices and shops as I neared the city centre. I would look for a jug first, to replace the one I had broken. There was a shop I was familiar with near Grafton Street that sold kitchen things and china; I would look there. I hoped to find something particular and unusual, something out of the common run, and I knew the kind of thing Molly liked. As I was going into the shop a woman and a teenage girl were coming out. I held the door open for them and she looked at me, a glance first, and a smile to thank me. Then she looked more acutely, and then she said my name aloud. Her face was vaguely familiar to me but I couldn't place her at all, and then she said her own name. 'Marian. Marian Dunne. Don't you remember me?'

'Marian!' I exclaimed. 'This is so strange. I was thinking about you only a couple of hours ago, thinking about when we were at college together.'

'And what put you in mind of me,' she said, 'after all these years?' That I didn't feel I could honestly answer, and I blustered a bit, made much of the coincidence of chance thoughts and a chance meeting. We moved aside from the door of the shop so as not to block it and the teenage girl – clearly Marian's daughter – withdrew to a slight distance from us, took out her mobile phone and started to check her texts.

Marian had always been blonde, and now she was resolutely so. The complicated arrangement of long hair had been replaced by a short, neat cut; and she was all gold chains and red lipstick, all crumpled white linen, with her sunglasses perched on the top of her head. She looked well; prosperous and *soignée*. It wasn't that she hadn't changed over the years, for she had; but what she had become in no way fell short of what I would have expected her to be at this time in her life. I thought of her gentle dismissal of Andrew all those years ago. *It's a pity.*

Weirdly then, before she asked after me or spoke about herself, she suddenly said, 'Tell me, Andrew Forde: do you still see him? I remember you were great friends altogether.' Was I becoming psychic? Was I able to summon up people merely by thinking about them? Could I plant thoughts in the minds of others? I told her that yes, Andrew and I had stayed in touch on and off over the years; we were still firm friends. 'Did you see him in the paper this morning? And his programme's on television tonight. I have all his books. He's done so well for himself, hasn't he? But of all people I would never have expected him to end up on television.' I told her that no one had been more surprised when it happened than Andrew himself, and she asked me how it had come about.

As an expert in the field, Andrew had been asked to present a five-minute film about a Bellini Crucifixion, in a little Easter series based on paintings. A tiny enterprise, it had been moving and powerful, not least because of Andrew's on-screen presence. Against a background of Charpentier's *Tenebrae* he didn't come across at all as a fusty pedant, his occasional self-deprecating description of himself. He wore his knowledge easily and was confident, relaxed. The film-makers picked up on his unexpected charisma and thought that it would be a waste for him to retreat back to his papers and paintings, to a life that was purely scholarly. They suggested a follow-up to him, an hour-long documentary about Giorgione, in which it was confirmed that Andrew was a natural for the small screen. Obviously I didn't say so to Marian, but this new development in his career had been something of an eye-opener for me. I had thought I knew Andrew very well indeed; I hadn't expected anything new to be revealed to me. But it was. There was something of himself he could communicate only in this way: not his considerable scholarship, but something else, some response to the work that was deeper, that was more than intellectual. I have never been able to define it, but I think that it was this unnameable thing, combined with his ability to be both populist and learned, that made him such a success in his new career. A series on portraits followed, together with a book, and then a similar project on landscape. I filled Marian in on the essence of this, the facts, and she listened, rapt.

'And you,' I said then. 'How are things with you?'

'Martin, do you remember Martin? He was studying medicine then. Well, I married him. He's a consultant now, a neurologist. We have two children. This is my daughter Sarah,' and she indicated the teenager, whose thumbs were flitting over the console of her phone. 'The boy, Thomas, is younger. He'll be thirteen on his next birthday. Did you ever marry?'

Two close shaves, three if you count Henry: bottled out of marrying Ken, with a week to go, because I knew it wouldn't work; bottled out of marrying Louis three years later, simply to punish myself for having bottled out the first time around. My love life deserves Molly's scorn.

'Me? No, I never married.'

'You're just right not to. I never thought you would anyway, you were always so into your theatre work. In any case so many marriages don't work out nowadays. Did I read somewhere that Andrew's divorced?' I nodded. What she said had affronted me, stung me, and I was tempted to walk away without another word. 'He has a son?' she persisted. 'He does,' I agreed.

'And you, you never had any children?'

'I would never want to have children without being married, and as I told you, that never happened,' I said. 'Terribly old-fashioned of me, I know.' She bit her lip and nodded, unsure as to whether or not I was being ironic.

'I'm still in Kildare,' she said suddenly. 'Can you believe it? All of my life, practically. I've got a part-time job with an interior designer, now that the children are half-grown. Advising on furniture, paintings, ceramics, that kind of thing. That's been my life: Kildare, Martin, the family.' In that instant she looked like someone who had awoken from a dream, the dream that was her life, and who saw it for the first time for what it was, how far it was from what she had imagined in the past it might become. She stared at me, more astounded by what she had just told me than she would have been by anything I could have told her. 'I'll give Andrew your best when next I see him,' I said, and she told me to be sure to do that. And then we went our separate ways.

I spent the first ten minutes in the shop looking blankly at kettles and thinking about Marian. Meeting her had been a dispiriting experience, as it so often can be when one meets old friends. The initial delight, the sense of connection, and then the distancing, the unravelling of that connection as information is exchanged and it becomes clear why one hasn't stayed in touch. Defensiveness sets in, and it all ends in melancholy when one is alone again. Then my eye fell on a thick pottery fruit bowl, spattered and dripped with colour, and I remembered why I had gone into the shop in the first place.

They had no ceramics I really liked; more to the point, nothing I thought would please Molly. I went to three more shops before I came on a cream-jug and sugar basin, a matching set in sponge-ware with a pattern of rose hips and little birds that was just what I wanted. From there I went to a bookshop, where the tables were piled high with books for the summer tourist trade – Joyce, Synge,

Beckett. I noticed a small gift volume of Wilde that would have appalled Oscar himself, for the jacket bore a design of peacock feathers. While this gave it a suitably stylish *fin de siècle* tone, it took no account of the fact that Wilde had a great superstitious fear of peacock feathers. And this little book would be no gift for Molly, because she shared the same fear. She had an argument once with a wardrobe mistress who wanted her to wear a dress adorned with peacock feathers; but it's a common enough superstition in the theatre, in itself a world riddled with such beliefs. The director backed Molly and the feathers were removed. I spent some time browsing in the book-shop but could see nothing that immediately suggested itself as something she would like.

I went to a café after that and had a mineral water out-side on the terrace with the smokers, even though I gave up cigarettes many years ago. I was tired from the crowds in the streets, tourists, Saturday shoppers; and the heat of the day was draining. Open-topped tour buses went past as I sat there and then a thing like a boat, a thing packed with children dressed as Vikings, who cheered as they went around the corner. I thought again about my encounter with Marian. I wondered how she would have reacted had it been Andrew she'd met by chance in the street, and I remembered his passion for her all those years ago. It was strange that someone whose need to worship was so intense could be so dismissive of religion.

The night his son Tony was born, for only the second time in all the years we've known each other, my friend-ship with Andrew crossed a certain line. Friendship is only that, friendship. There are areas of reserve and dis-tance, knowledge and experience that cannot be shared or entered into. When these limits are not observed, it stops being friendship and starts being something else. I was the first person Andrew rang from the maternity hospital. Tony was born in the depths of the night, sometime after 4 a.m., the hour of the wolf, the hour of dreams and nightmares, of deepest sleep. The phone call caught me then with no conscious defences whatsoever, the incessant ringing frightened me at such an hour. There was a man crying on the other end of the line, and then he said my name and I knew it was Andrew. 'What's wrong? What's happening?' He told me that his son had just been born. Coming straight from the delivery room, he was in a strange state of extreme emotional openness; and in my own night-time confusion I more than matched him. If he was like someone who had been caught up in an explosion, I was like a hibernating animal that had been accidentally woken out of a sleep that was close to coma. Nicole was fine, the baby was fine, he had never imagined . . . he didn't know . . . Had he rung me like this, babbling and weeping, at four in the afternoon rather than four in the morning, I'd probably have reacted with cool amusement. I'm very glad things didn't work out that way, and Tony's birth became an emotionally charged moment of connection between Andrew and myself, unique, intimate, something we have never spoken of again to each other from that day to this. Andrew was still sobbing and close to incoherent when he hung up. I crashed back into sleep almost immediately, and when I awoke in the morning the memory of the whole thing was like a bizarre dream.

I went to the maternity hospital the following day. Nicole was sitting up in bed holding the baby, with

Andrew on a chair leaning in towards them, to form a version of one of his beloved paintings: a secular nativity. Nicole's little face was pale and shut as a Flemish Madonna; the baby was absurdly small, out of proportion with the rest of the scene; and Andrew gazed at the pair of them in frank adoration, the ecstatic patron experiencing a vision. As the years passed and Tony grew, I realised that Andrew had at last found an object worthy of his devotion, someone who would return his wholly unconditional love.

Andrew's mother died and was long buried before I heard about it, for I was abroad when it happened, but I did attend his father's funeral, about five years after Tony was born. I found out quite by chance that he was dead, when I decided for no particular reason one day to speak to Andrew. We had drifted apart a bit in those years of his marriage, mainly because Nicole and I didn't get on. On the rare occasions when I did ring him, I had taken to calling him at work to avoid having to speak to her. 'Mr Forde won't be in for the rest of the week,' his assistant told me, 'his father passed away this morning.' I made a snap decision to be at the funeral, even though I was particularly busy with work at that time. It was easy enough to find out where and when it was taking place. I cancelled two meetings and booked a flight, arranged to pick up a hire car at Belfast airport. My plan was to be over and back within the day, which was eminently possible.

I was nervous as I went into the church. Although in London I had attended funerals in traditions with which I was unfamiliar, in Ireland I had only ever been to Catholic ceremonies. Andrew's family was Church of Ireland. It was a small funeral and most of the mourners were elderly. As I sat waiting for the service to begin I looked around the church, admiring it: the great brass lectern in the shape of an eagle, the lustre of the tiled floor, cream and ochre and dark green. With a start I realised that this must be the church Andrew told me about, the first beautiful thing he had ever seen. I hoped that he would remember that today, and that it might afford him some comfort.

Andrew came into the church just before the funeral began, with Nicole walking a short distance behind him. The service was short, with a few hymns and readings from the Bible, using the King James Version, which was unfamiliar to me. It distanced and made strange familiar texts – the sufferings of Job, the raising of Lazarus – but the grave beauty of the language also enhanced them. The minister spoke at some length about Andrew's father, whom he had attended in the hospital in the final weeks of his life, and whom he referred to as 'Andy'. I hadn't known until then that Andrew had been named after his father. The minister said that Andy had lived the last twenty years of his life under the burden of a sorrow so great as to be nigh on unbearable: the death, indeed the murder, of his beloved son Billy. He likened Andrew's father to King David, whose cries rang through the palace as he grieved for Absalom: *O my son Absalom, my son, my son Absalom! Would I had died instead of you, O Absalom, my son, my son!* He said that Andy, his late wife Rose and their loving and dutiful son Andrew, who was here with us today, were all fully victims of the Troubles, and that they had borne with fortitude their terrible loss. Andrew's devotion to Andy had been moving to see, he said; his solicitude, his many visits back to

Belfast particularly in this last year of his father's life. Now Andy's grief was over, now he was at peace. Something was at an end, but it was also a new beginning. Then we said a few more prayers, there was another hymn, and it was all over.

Afterwards I stood outside the church, ill at ease amongst the mourners who gathered in groups talking to each other. There was no one I recognised, no one I knew except Nicole. She was also standing on her own, but when I caught her eye and started to move towards her, she gave no hint of recognition. It was as if she had never seen me before and had no wish to get acquainted. I abandoned my attempt to approach her. Instead, I joined a small huddle of people who were gathered around Andrew, taking their turn to shake his hand and offer their sympathy. Most of them were elderly: friends and neighbours of his parents; old work colleagues of his father's. I was finding the whole day ineffably depressing, much more so than I had expected. I had come out of loyalty to Andrew, but the deep sorrow of the occasion, which the minister had skilfully identified, was getting to me. I waited for the last few people gathered around Andrew to disperse. It was November, but at least it was a dry, bright day, the sky all blue and the ground covered with fallen leaves. And then Andrew saw me.

He hadn't realised until then that I was present at the funeral, and it was clearly a great surprise to him. I tried to say a few words of condolence, but it was beyond me. He said my name; he said it again, and then he enveloped me in a great brotherly bear hug, crushing me and holding me to himself for some moments, so that my face was buried in the soft darkness of his overcoat. It was the first heartfelt gesture I had seen him make, the first real emotion he had shown all morning. I was overcome by it too, for it was out of character for Andrew and me, who were usually so undemonstrative with each other. When, as a part of the package of new social rituals he had adopted on moving to England, he took to giving me a little kiss when we met, he knew I found it slightly false, and although we still greeted each other in this way, it was usually with a degree of irony on both sides.

'I can't tell you how much it means to me to see you here today,' he said. I did then manage a few words of sympathy. I told him I was glad that, from what the minister said, Andrew and his father had drawn closer towards the end. 'Did we?' he said. 'I don't know. We spent a lot of time together, as much as I could manage, but did we get close to each other? I don't know. Close: what does that even mean? Maybe that's the answer. It's not just my father's passing. It's like the death of a whole family now, with both parents gone as well as Billy.'

'You're still here,' I said stupidly.

'Not for long. I'll still have to come back and forth for a while to wrap things up: sell the house, close a couple of bank accounts, that kind of thing. In all honesty, there isn't a great deal to see to. And after that, my most ardent wish is never to come back to Belfast, ever, ever again.'

The undertakers were still preparing the hearse for departure. I asked Andrew about the burial and he said to me, 'Don't even think about attending it. You've already done more than enough by being here today. Are you going back to London tonight? Let me walk you to your car. Where are you parked?'

As we crossed the short distance around the side of the

church towards the hire car he said, 'Did you have a word with Nicole?'

'I'm afraid not.'

'I wouldn't worry about it. She's barely speaking to me these days. I was surprised she agreed to come over to the funeral. I don't think we're going to make it.' And then because he could see the look of bewilderment on my face he added, 'I know, I can hardly believe it myself.'

'But Tony –' I began, and he winced.

'I know, I know. That's for another day. I just wanted you to know what the situation was.' It felt like another death. Looking at Andrew I could see how hard it went with him. We didn't speak again until we reached the car, and then I told him to ring me when he was back in London and had settled. We would meet for a drink, or have lunch together. He thanked me once more for coming to the funeral and we said goodbye. He put his arms around me and embraced me again, but this time without the sudden, rib-crushing intensity. It was a strange embrace, caught somewhere between friendship and sensuality, for he kissed me on the cheek, but slowly, tenderly. He held me in his arms for a few moments and stroked my hair before kissing me once more. And then, rather awkwardly, he let me go.

I had left the city far behind me and was well on the way to the airport when I pulled over to the side of the road and took out my phone. I extended the car hire by an extra day and postponed the flight until late the following evening. It was only after I'd made these arrangements that I began to think about what I might do with this extra time. I only knew that it was too soon for me to go back to London: I wasn't ready to do that. I needed time to assimilate everything that the morning had brought forth. Above all, I could see now the great failure of imagination there had been on my part in not understanding what Billy's death had meant. I hadn't realised that such a tragedy wasn't fixed in the past, but was an active, malignant thing, that changed and mutated over the years; and it never went away. I had taken at face value Andrew's silence over the years, and in this I had been foolish. The minister was right, there was something biblical in the family's loss. *A certain man had two sons.* The lost son, murdered; and then the living son with whom he would never be reconciled, not in this life: and Andrew believed in no other.

I suppose it goes without saying that I headed for home. That is, I drove over to where my family lived. I went by the most circuitous route and I took my time. I thought about Andrew the whole way there. It seemed an irony that I had rarely seen the north looking lovelier than it was today. The light deepened and intensified – a rich gold that lit up the landscape, the fading trees and the hedges with their bright berries; the drenched, flooded fields. To me it was a tragic place; to Andrew it had always been simply wretched. Perhaps he was right after all, I thought now, and in taking the view I did I was according it a sad poetry that it not only didn't merit, but that was a real perversion, romanticising all that had happened there. 'Dark feelings can become a habit,' he'd said to me once when we were talking – arguing – about this. 'And if they're strong enough, like many strong feelings they can even be enjoyable.' He said that this was why the peace process wasn't working, that the whole population was locked in a trance of grief that they didn't break out of because it defined them, it made them feel real. And in talking about all this he never once mentioned Billy.

I crested the brow of a hill, and there below me were the mountains of mid-Ulster, low and ancient, with their soft skyline. Blue-grey, green, on and on they went across the whole of the wide horizon, but gentle, for all that. There was a quietude about them that I loved to see, and that made them dearer to me than other, more spectacular mountain ranges. The sun was setting on them now as the short day ended. To me these mountains said one thing above all: home. At this precise moment, this was where I needed to be. I pulled the car over again and sat staring at the landscape before me. Where was I to stay tonight? I thought of my married sisters, my brothers' families. I knew that even showing up unannounced I would be welcome; the inconvenience would mean nothing to them. But I wouldn't be able to bear it today, the babies, the dinners cooking, the television blaring in the background, the cloying happiness of it all and of which I would never fully be a part. I would go to Tom's house instead. If he wasn't there or couldn't accommodate me it didn't matter; I would find a hotel or a guest house. It was enough that I had been here today. I needed that.

Tom was a parish priest now. His church was surrounded by a small graveyard, and beyond that was the parochial house, where he lived alone. It was deep in the countryside, about half a mile from the nearest house and three miles from the nearest village. It dated from a time long before the falling off in vocations to the priesthood, and at one time a curate and a housekeeper would have lived there, as well as the parish priest. Now there was only Tom. The house was grey and forbidding, a stern square block; and only a few rather lovely lime trees surrounding the church softened the impact of all that stone; of the granite crosses in the graveyard.

Tom was astonished when he opened the door and found me standing on the step; worried too, for he thought something must be wrong. I quickly reassured him and explained the situation. He told me there would be no problem with my staying the night, that he would be glad to have some unexpected time with me. 'I have to say Mass at seven o'clock this evening, but other than that I have no commitments. There's always the possibility I'll be called out, but I had to go to an accident at four this morning, so I'm hoping not to be disturbed tonight.' We were in the kitchen by now and Tom was making tea. We moved from there up to the sitting room, where a fire was lit in the grate. It reassured me, this room, after the austerity of the outside of the house. It was warm and full of books. On the floor beside the stereo there was a scattering of CDs that Tom hadn't bothered to put back in their cases. This untidiness compensated for the slightly institutional air the room, indeed the whole house, had, that was afforded by the presence of a few religious pictures and statues and by something else that I could never quite define.

'This funeral you were at in Belfast,' he said, 'whose was it?' He knew who I meant when I mentioned Andrew, for I had spoken of him from time to time over the years. I explained the situation in some detail and told him about Billy too, about Tony and Nicole. Tom listened. 'Is Andrew religious at all?' he asked when I'd finished.

'He isn't, no.'

'That's a pity.'

'He wouldn't see it that way. He's against the very idea of religion, to be honest with you.'

'Do you ever talk to him about it?' I hadn't for years, not since I was a student, for I was no longer sure enough of what I myself believed. I didn't want to expose my last poor, weak vestiges of faith to the brisk rationality of Andrew's atheism, but I wasn't going to tell Tom that.

'No, I don't,' I said, 'but himself and Molly row about it from time to time. It can get quite heated, vehement, you know.' Tom laughed.

'I bet it can. What sort of thing does Molly say?'

'Oh, I can't remember now.'

'How's she keeping these days?'

'You tell me,' I was tempted to reply, for this was at a time when I still faintly resented their friendship. I had begun to realise that Molly had a much stronger personality than I did, for all her shyness and (at times) mousy demeanour. She had a habit of taking over my friends, my family, now, even, as a cat will quietly move into the warm, empty chair one has vacated, and refuse to give it up again.

'Molly's fine,' I said. 'Busy as always.'

'She said an interesting thing to me a while back,' Tom remarked. 'We were talking about her work and she said that there's a kind of truth that can only be expressed through artifice. She said that what she wanted to convey to people through her work, more than anything else, was reality. It was a question of showing something familiar but in a moment outside time; saying, "Here's love, here's sorrow. Do you recognise them?" I thought it was a good way of putting it.'

More than Tom, I appreciated the accuracy of what

Molly had said, because unlike him I had worked in the theatre. I knew the force of the experience one might have as a member of an audience; but I also knew intimately the strange tawdriness of the things that made it happen: the dressing rooms with their stale air and harshly lit mirrors; those blank corridors and stairways backstage; the faint smell of dust and sweat from old costumes. At no time does a play look more unconvincing than when viewed from the wings, but Molly had laughed when I said this to her. 'It looks even more peculiar when you're on stage in the middle of it, believe me.'

'Do the family know you're here?' he said suddenly.

'No.' He let a silence sit between us for me to fill. 'I couldn't face it, Tom, and I don't know why.'

'You can get too much of a good thing,' he said, after another long pause. 'I won't let on that you've been here.'

'I feel guilty about it.'

'There's no reason. Conventional life always expects you to meet it more than halfway. You should give yourself the benefit of the doubt from time to time.' There was another long silence which he finally broke himself, by adding, 'I certainly do.'

Later in the evening, when the time had come for him to go over to the church, he suggested that I stay at home. It was a Wednesday-night Mass in November; it would be simple and quite short, with no music or sermon. He wouldn't be gone for long. 'Read the paper, why don't you, or watch television.' But as soon as I was on my own the atmosphere of the house began to unsettle me. I was too conscious of the many dark, empty rooms. The silence was so complete that the coals settling in the grate startled me; and when I put on music I wondered what strange sounds it might be drowning out. At ten to seven I banked up the fire, put on my coat and let myself out into the night.

All the lights from within the church pressed against the coloured windows, so that the building itself looked like a reliquary or some kind of remarkable shrine. The stained glass glowed; its pictures of saints and angels were vibrant and fragile. Once inside, this effect was lost. The church was nothing like as interesting architecturally as the one in Belfast where the funeral had taken place that morning. It was like a great many other churches I had known during my life. There were the usual banks of little candles before plaster statues. The altar was decorated with some tough, long-lasting white flowers, carnations and chrysanthemums. The windows now looked black, with only the faintest of images visible if one studied them with particular attention. A small congregation had assembled. As I waited for the Mass to start, some of Molly's arguments in favour of belief came back to me.

It wasn't so much a question of believing in a certain thing as not being able to believe in certain other things, and so finding faith by default. She said that much as she valued it, she could never believe in society as a final truth, and the arbitrator of morality. What convinced her in the gospels was the constant denial of the world, that is, of worldliness; she liked the strange, unfathomable and elliptical remarks Christ made. She believed in a consciousness that encompassed everything; compassionate, forgiving. When she argued with Andrew, I noticed something strange: that what he understood as religion and rejected was far more orthodox and narrow than what she believed in, so that they were always talking at cross purposes. He was more concerned with the lack of material proof than she was. You could pray for a miracle, he said, but it would never happen. The blind stayed blind, the lame, lame. And why, Molly answered, would one be so foolish as to pray for a miracle? It got to the stage when she wouldn't talk to him about it at all; when religion came up she immediately changed the subject.

The door of the sacristy opened and Tom came out. He rang a small golden bell that was suspended from the wall, and crossed to the altar. The congregation stood up and the Mass began.

I remembered all the responses, knew when to stand, to sit and to kneel, in spite of not having been to Mass for longer than I could remember. I didn't – and don't – equate art with religion, but what struck me that evening was the theatrical nature of what I was seeing. At times, it was all I could do to stop myself from applauding. There was that same contrast between the energy and significance of what was taking place and the shabby props that went towards it – those cheap flowers, the banality of the stylised lamb embroidered on the vestments Tom was wearing.

I was torn in my attitude to Catholicism and most of the time, I suppose, I tried not to think about it. Tonight, that wasn't an option. I would never be able to turn my back on it completely, nor would I ever be able to feel wholeheartedly at ease within it. Perhaps that didn't matter. Perhaps Molly was right and, like Andrew, I was taking too narrow and orthodox a definition of religion and then feeling bothered because I couldn't come to terms with it. Tom crossed to the lectern. The second reading was from the Book of Revelation. *Would that you were cold or hot! So, because you are lukewarm, and neither cold nor hot, I will spew you out of my mouth*. Well, I thought, that's me told. He prayed for someone in the parish who had been killed in an accident early that morning, and for her family. Stripped to its essentials, without hymns or a sermon, the Mass had an austere beauty that I hadn't expected. Tom let short periods of silence fall from time to time. Someone rang another little bell. We knelt and he performed the rite of consecration. When everyone else went up to Communion, I didn't join them.

When the final prayers had been said, I remained in my pew until the congregation had departed, until Tom opened the sacristy doors and beckoned to me. He switched off the last lights in the church as I approached him, and was putting on his coat as I entered the sacristy, with its strange clutter of ecclesiastical bric-a-brac, censers and candlesticks and incense boats. 'Isn't this a tremendously cheerless place?' he remarked to me moments later, as he locked the main door of the church. 'I'll never forget the first day I saw it; that big gloomy house, so isolated. I thought, "How am I going to live here?"' We turned to pick our way through the darkness of the graveyard. 'There was a housekeeper some years back and she swore the place was haunted, which is rubbish of course, but I can see where she got the idea.'

Back in the sitting room, we stoked the fire again and coaxed it into brilliant flames. 'What's it like as a parish?' I asked.

'Oh, it's very difficult. The priest who was here before me, he was an arrogant man. I hate to have to say that, but he created a lot of bad feeling and hostility towards the Church, and those wounds are still there.'

'That woman you prayed for,' I said, 'the woman who died: is that the road accident you were called to this morning?' He nodded.

'She wasn't a woman. She was only a young girl; she was seventeen. She died in hospital a couple of hours later. You don't want to know about it.'

'Were you at the scene of the accident or at the hospital?'

'Both. You *really* don't want to know about it.' Tom was the most squeamish person I knew. He covered his face if even the mildest of medical scenes came on television. It was something of a standing joke in our family. *Open-heart surgery on BBC 2 tonight. Set the video, Tom.*

'How do you do it?' I asked. He knew what I meant.

'No choice. Comes with the territory. Girl's parents had no choice either. They're the ones to feel sorry for, not me.' There was a long pause, and then he literally shuddered at the memory. 'Let's talk about something else.'

But we didn't talk at all. He lay back in his chair and closed his eyes. Within a few moments, I realised that he'd fallen asleep, and I sat very still so as not to wake him. 'And how are you?' he'd asked me earlier that day. I'd known it wasn't a casual question, a mere politeness. Sometimes I wished I could have him simply as a brother, without the priestly thing, but that was a vain hope. When I tried to follow the wish by imagining that brother, I drew a blank, so integral was his calling to his identity. He didn't pry into my life, he wasn't judgemental, but he ministered constantly, to me, to Molly, to anyone who crossed his path. Even when I'd spoken to him of Andrew and his family I could see his deep engagement, that concern that was both profound and detached. Emotion was of less concern to him than was usual with most people. He'd asked how I was, not how I was feeling. 'Never mind me, Tom. How are *you*?'

The prevailing orthodoxy denigrated what he was, saw it at best as irrelevant, at worst as inherently corrupt. It was the strangest life you could imagine. There was, to begin with, so much bureaucracy and administration, the number-crunching practicality of running a parish that he admitted to finding deeply enervating. There was much that was merely social. His priestly duties were considerable, Masses, funerals, christenings and the like. Ten pounds, my mother told me he'd been offered recently to officiate at a wedding. *And when you think of what they spend on flowers, on photographs . . .* But no matter what the world thought of him nor how shabbily it treated him, Tom stayed faithful to the impulse that had led him into this calling in the first place. That he was able to do this was what made his life strange: the interaction between so much quotidian reality and his pure heart.

As I was sitting at the café terrace, drinking my mineral water and thinking about all this, a bus pulled up on the other side of the road. On its side, between the upper and lower deck, was a long narrow poster advertising a new movie. Against the title and a background of flames were the faces of an impossibly beautiful woman in profile, and a man who was staring straight out of the poster, with a hunted look that only enhanced his glamour. David McKenzie. There was no great surprise in seeing him like this. In the years since I had first met him, I had become accustomed to the sight of David's face on bus shelters, on vast hoardings, on the front of glossy magazines. The green eyes had become iconic. It was now something of a cliché to photograph him with much of his face masked or obscured – one vivid eye was enough to convey his image, his whole self, so recognisable had he become, so famous. I think I would have been surprised, rather, had he failed to become a celebrity, given the nature of his gift, his personality and his looks. This last, whilst important, was not the most important factor. It was the way everything came together; the way the camera and the screen loved him, as they disdained Molly, the finer actor.

One evening, only a couple of years ago, Molly and I had been in a cinema together, waiting for a film to begin, when a trailer came on for the latest David McKenzie vehicle. Pretty well all his films are action movies with a bit of love interest, and this new one fitted the pattern. There were shots of David abseiling down the side of a building; of a car exploding; of David running; of him holding a sleek silver pistol that looked like a fashion accessory rather than a weapon; of a darkly beautiful woman in a tight red dress who was also holding a gun and who whispered in a generic foreign accent, 'Don't think I wouldn't kill you.' David's improbable reaction to this was to kiss her passionately. All of these images were speedily intercut with captions – *A mystery he must solve. A love he cannot escape. A past he cannot leave behind* – with the names of the actors and the title of the film, all read aloud in doomy tones by someone who sounded as if he was speaking from the bottom of a deep trench. I regarded this kind of tosh with humour and affection when David was involved. I turned to Molly and said, 'I might just go along and see this one, for David. For old times' sake.' She didn't respond. She was still staring at the screen, where he had just jumped straight through a plate-glass window in slow motion, and then she said, 'If he'd asked me, I'd have married him.' I thought about this for a minute. 'But he is married,' I said stupidly. 'He was always married.' She turned and looked at me. 'Of course he is,' she said, with a note of annoyance in her voice. 'But you know what I mean.'

Did I? The trailers were over and the advertisements were beginning now, heralded by the image of a star-shaped branding iron being pulled out of smouldering coals and seemingly thrust towards the screen. This was typical of Molly: the earth-shattering piece of information turned into a throwaway remark and delivered at the wrong time, in an incongruous place. *My brother is in a mental hospital. If I never had to see my mother again, it would suit me fine. If he'd asked me, I'd have married him.* Molly was looking intently at the screen, as if these advertisements mattered to her, as if she might actually want to buy a Coke or a Land Cruiser, as if she was seriously considering joining the army. The branding iron appeared again, the lights went down fully, and the film began.

I couldn't concentrate on the movie, whatever it was, for thinking about what she had said. Not for a moment did I doubt the veracity of her statement. It was the implications that confounded me.

Molly doesn't do intimacy. Who was it who had made this telling remark? Not me, not David, certainly not Andrew. It was Fergus. Fergus of all people, Molly's beloved brother. He said it one day when the three of us were together in her house, and she had made some remark about 'an intimate friend' just as she was leaving the room to fetch something. He waited until she was out of earshot and then he said to me, 'Intimate friend? As if. Molly doesn't do intimacy.' Fergus, I had realised not long after I met him, for all that he was vulnerable, for all that he was intermittently troubled and depressed, knew and understood Molly to a degree that was slightly unnerving. Until I got to know him well, I expected very little from Fergus. I defined him by his distress, and it took me a long time to work out that this was a mistake; longer still to realise that my initial view was one that Molly encouraged, that she had even planted the idea in my head. Fergus's shaky emotional life concealed a sharp mind. He would make the odd aperçu that surprised me until I thought about it and saw it to be both accurate and profound, as was the case here. The closer you get to Molly, the more she seems to recede. Sometimes she seems to me like a figure in a painting, the true likeness of a woman, but as you approach the canvas the image breaks up, becomes fragmented into the colours, the brushstrokes and the daubs of paint from which the thing itself is constructed. Only by withdrawing can the illusion be effected again. Molly wants to be remote.

What she does do, instead of intimacy, is love. She loves Fergus, for example, to a degree that I find hard to comprehend: an intense, visceral, *Nelly, I am Heathcliff* kind of love in which the personalities, the very souls of the people involved seem to melt into each other. I can't follow her there and I don't want to. That kind of love frightens me.

She loves Tom, my brother, too. I know this because she told me one day when she was showing me one of his little gifts, a candle in a holder of blue stained glass. 'I love Tom,' she said as she replaced the candle on the shelf. I knew she meant it because it was lightly said; and it was not an expression she used casually. Never would she use it about any of her passing boyfriends. *He's a laugh. He's great fun. I'm very fond of him. He's a decent bloke, good company. I'm glad he's around.* I even dared to mention this once to Tom himself. 'Molly really loves you, you know,' and I think his reply was just what I would have expected. 'That's sweet of her. She's very endearing.' By this time I felt more sure about the link that there was between them, even though neither of them had ever said a word to me about it.

In speaking of Marian, I mentioned a man named Louis whom I almost married. That I ultimately refused to do so was, and remains, the single most foolish act in a life not wanting in errors of judgement. Louis was a set designer, a gentle soul with whom I could have had a happy life. I know that now. But here's the rub: I knew it at the time and yet I insisted on breaking up with him. Afterwards, I was bewildered by the way I had behaved. What was the source of this desire to act against my own best interests? My own actions and motivation were so unfathomable to me that I decided only therapy could help. I wanted to understand and, to use the relevant jargon, move on with my life.

Of the many books on Molly's shelves, I doubt if there's a single one concerning psychology. It is a subject of which she has an innate and profound understanding, and she brings it to bear upon her acting. The psychological depth and accuracy of her work is something that is frequently remarked upon and praised. And yet towards psychology as a discipline, towards any structured approach to it, she is at best indifferent and at worst hostile. She attempted to talk me out of what I was planning.

The therapist's office was furnished with such quiet good taste that it resembled the home of someone with no personality whatsoever. Magnolia walls. Cut flowers. A framed print of a painting by Raoul Dufy. A wide desk with a jug of water on it, two glasses and a box of tissues. I went there every Wednesday morning for months on end. It became a black hole in the middle of my week, a desolate appointment with the aspects of myself I least liked, and I grew to dread it. The therapist was a woman of about my own age – I was then in my early thirties – but more *soignée* and elegant than I would ever even aspire to be. She wore cashmere, pearls and little tailored suits in pastel colours. I paid her a fortune, drank the water from the jug, and snuffled my way through many tissues as we speculated tirelessly on the root and cause of my problems. We considered my family, my position therein, my mother, my father, my siblings and my relations with them, Ken, Louis, and even my childhood sweetheart, poor old Henry, the fact of whose existence she winkled out of me. (The therapist thought that Henry was particularly significant and that in disagreeing with this judgement I was in denial.) I rarely left the room feeling better about the situation than I had done when I arrived, and any shred of insight gained lasted only until the next session, when it would all be unpicked and unravelled like incompetent knitting, and a new source of woe would be speculated upon.

Eventually we began to focus upon my career, which the therapist thought highly suspect and perhaps as significant a source of trouble as Henry. Her theory was that the creation of different characters in the course of writing plays was, in essence, the creation of multiple selves. I asked her if she was suggesting that this was an expression of dissatisfaction with my real self. She smiled at me pityingly and said, 'Your "real" self? Ah, if only such a thing existed!' I told her that while I was at times as riddled with anxiety and insecurity about my work as any writer, concerning my identity as a playwright I was in no doubt whatsoever. It was the one area in which I would brook no question, the one matter in which I was impregnable. Even in moments when I wasn't actively engaged upon writing plays, being a playwright was what I was. I could see that she thought I was being obtuse. She also thought I was being self-aggrandising, and I tried to clarify what I meant by admitting that it was quite possible that I wasn't a particularly good playwright. Indeed there would be days when I would be the first to admit that this was the case. (Today, Molly's birthday, was a perfect example of such a day.) The therapist declared that she had finally found the cause of all my troubles in life, but that my stubborn denial of it would first have to be broken down. 'We have a great deal of work ahead of us,' she said as I was leaving at the end of that session. 'It will require considerable courage on your part.' I politely agreed and left the building, knowing that I would never return.

It so happened that Molly was in London the following weekend. She knew by my demeanour that something was up, and she wouldn't rest until she had coaxed out of me what had happened. 'I feared this,' she said, when I had explained the situation. 'I thought that this would never work because I believed that there was never anything much wrong with you in the first place, nothing that time and life itself won't sort out.' In all of this she was much more sympathetic than I would have expected. I remember clearly how she looked as she spoke to me. She was wearing a plain black woollen dress with a silver pin in it. Her brown eyes were soft and she was thoughtful, sombre. 'I regret now having been so forceful in trying to dissuade you. But believe me, if you'd been like Fergus, I'd have been the first to help you, to make sure you got proper treatment. Doctors. A good psychiatrist.'

'I know that, Molly,' I soothed her. I could see that the subject was distressing her and I understood why. Her mother's departure when she was seven was not something that I thought about often, and when I did I associated it more with Fergus than with Molly.

I soon realised that Molly had been right all along. Time and life itself sorted me out. I awoke the following Wednesday morning feeling light-hearted, elated to know that I would be spending no portion of the day, nor indeed any time ever again in the future, in the magnolia room with that woman. I threw myself into my work, finished a new play, was involved in the successful revival of an earlier work, and then began rehearsals for the new piece. I started a new relationship and, unusually for me, one of the things I liked about it was that I knew it wouldn't last. Right from the beginning I could sense that the end of this particular affair was hardwired into it and – this was a new idea to me – it only made it all the sweeter while it lasted. And in this way I got over Louis. Molly approved hugely. There has always been much about me that she considers quaint, but to know this has never bothered me in the least. Such a friendship can provide good checks and balances in life. In particular she has always found my idea that marriage might be the end-station of any given connection to be hopelessly out-moded, which made her remark in the cinema about David McKenzie all the more surprising.

I had met David again a couple of years before that for the first time since we had worked together, me and Molly and David and Ken, back in the early days. I had arrived for a meeting at a hotel in central London to find that David and a few of his fellow actors were upstairs giving press interviews about their latest film. Although I knew he would be working to a tight schedule and that it would be all but impossible to penetrate the mass of PR people, minders and assistants who surrounded him in situations like this, I put in a request to see if it would be possible to meet. The publicist to whom I spoke seemed to recognise my name and said that she couldn't promise anything, but would see what she could do. And so it came about that at the end of the afternoon, when we had both fin-ished our meetings, I was ushered into his presence.

'Isn't this incredible?' he cried, jumping up from his chair when he saw me. 'I couldn't believe it when they said you were here.' The room was all gold and white, with fake Louis XV furniture and elaborate curtains, looped and fringed. I wished our meeting might have hap-pened elsewhere: in its own way this place was as anony-mous as the therapist's room had been, but this was the world in which David now lived. He kissed me, settled me in a chair beside a display of roses and lilies, arranged for drinks to be sent up, and said again, 'This is incredible.'

And it was. All the time I was talking to him, and we were together for just over an hour, I was aware of a kind of parallax, of how he loomed and receded before me, my view of him changing on the moment by some imperceptible means. Sometimes I was acutely aware of his being David McKenzie, the celebrity, the star he had become, whose image was familiar from Manhattan to Malawi. In the next instant he was again just David, the kind-hearted, easy-going actor with whom I had worked many years ago. There was no initial awkwardness to be got over. Meeting him again was a far more comfortable experience than meeting Marian was to be. There was no point-scoring, no prickliness; neither of us was using the other to defend our position or bolster our own short-comings. I was no threat to David, and he had nothing to prove. At my insistence we talked a bit about his new film. Laughing, self-deprecating, he dismissed it. It was another piece of hokum, this time about aliens and computer hacking, and then I dared to ask him if he ever thought about going back to the theatre. 'I'd love that,' he said, 'but it's not going to happen. I've burnt my boats on that one.' I protested that lots of film actors were returning to the stage, but he shook his head. 'It wouldn't work,' he said. 'The kind of people who like to watch my movies don't want to see Chekhov, and the kind of people who like Chekhov don't want to see me. It definitely wouldn't work but I'm not complaining. I made my choice years ago and I'm happy to stand by it. You can't have everything in life.'

Perhaps not, but as we talked more I realised that David came as close to it as was possible. He was still with Mel, and they had three children now, 'American kids,' he said, amused at the idea. They'd moved to the States when his film career began to take off; it had made perfect sense, and had worked out better than he had ever dared hope. They got home from time to time to see their families back in England, but more often than not David's parents and Mel's came and stayed with them. He wasn't telling me anything I hadn't read a dozen times in newspapers and celebrity magazines: his contented home life was legendary.

But then that imperceptible shift took place again, like a piece of coloured glass slipping within a kaleidoscope, and everything changed. Sitting before me, green-eyed, handsome, smiling, was that rare thing: a happy man. The glittering career was beside the point. Here was someone whose mother hadn't walked out on him when he was seven. He didn't have a traumatised brother, nor one who was his bitter rival. He wasn't a misfit, someone who was the product of a stable background but who simply couldn't fit into it, and whose whole life and work was an effort to understand this failure to connect. He wasn't compensating for anything. David was fortunate and he knew it; he would frankly admit as much if you asked him. His gift was mimesis and it was considerable. He could act out grief, fear, love, anything he was called upon to present. He couldn't have been more unlike Molly, whose soul and art were full of darkness. Why did I feel such pathos as I talked to him? Not for his own sake but for the way in which he was a bright field, that set all the rest of us in relief. The time was racing past. I wanted to stay in his presence. He asked me about my own life, my work, my family; we talked about the film industry, the theatre, about Molly, Ken. I'd have been happy to talk to him about the weather. An assistant appeared at the door and reminded him about another appointment elsewhere. He sent her away, saying he would be ready in a moment. We talked for another quarter of an hour but when the assistant came back again briefly, looking peeved, I knew that I really ought to go.

We stood up to take our leave of each other. He confidently enfolded me into a great warm bear-hug, and it embarrasses me to admit that I was completely thrown by this and that I pretty much collapsed into his embrace. I clung to him for some moments with my head on his shoulder; I didn't want to let him go. David reacted with aplomb, as well he might, having stage-managed this moment. If Molly didn't do intimacy, clearly David didn't do anything else.

I had remembered all of this as I sat there in the cinema with her; I thought of how it would be difficult to find two people more dissimilar. 'Molly,' I said to her when the lights came up at the end, 'it would never have worked. You must realise that.'

She looked at me blankly. 'What are you talking about?'

'You and David McKenzie.'

'Of course it wouldn't have worked. I didn't say that it would have, did I? Really and truly!' She gave a little snort of exasperation as if I was being incredibly obtuse, which of course I was.

While I'd been thinking about him the bus bearing David's image had long since disappeared. By now it would be far out of the city centre, out by the sea, out where I'd been living at the time when Andrew had stayed with me, just before he left for England. It was mid-afternoon by now. I left the café and looked in a few more bookshops for a while, then I did some food shopping. I had some coffee beans weighed and ground for a percolator. In a shop fronted by a display of stacked, tilted wooden crates I bought grapes and tomatoes, salad and strawberries. From an elaborate display of fish in shattered ice, heaped on marble, I selected a piece of cod, and then I realised that I hadn't thought through any of this, that I should have bought parsley and a lemon earlier to go with the fish. I was taking a scattergun approach, stringing things out because I didn't much want to go home, but in the strange, remembering, slightly melancholy frame of mind I was in I couldn't think of anything else I would be able to settle on. I had checked the paper earlier and there was nothing in the cinema I wanted to see. I knew that, preoccupied as I was, I wouldn't be able to focus on looking at paintings. When I had dragged out the shopping for as long as possible I headed back to the house, but even then I took a long, illogical route, passing through Stephen's Green.

There were people everywhere, draped out on the grass in the sunshine, talking and laughing, small children feeding the ducks. Molly had once remarked that in her experience every city had places that were particularly psychically charged, that they were the focus of odd energies and that strange things happened there – highly unusual encounters and connections, remarkable coincidences – and that in Dublin Stephen's Green was such a place. Fergus was there when she said this, and he laughed out loud. 'You're talking rubbish, Molly. It's a park, a public space. If odd things happen there, that's why. They could just as easily occur in any public place.'

'But they don't.'

'They do! All the time,' he insisted.

'Not when you're just walking down the street.'

'Parks are like hotels. The very nature of what they provide allows the kind of thing you're talking about to happen.' They asked me then to adjudicate, and I sided with Fergus, for I did think what Molly was arguing was fanciful. But about six months later something happened that made me not so sure.

I was back in Dublin for a brief visit and was to stay with Molly. I took the coach in from the airport and got off in O'Connell Street. As was so often the case, she would be coming from another meeting which was in that part of the city, and she had suggested that I wait for her in a nearby hotel with which I was unfamiliar. Tucked away in a side-street, it was shabby and unfashionable, and I liked the look of it immediately for that very reason. It struck me as a place where you would be most unlikely to bump into someone you knew, which made it appealing in a city where anonymity was so often in short supply. I sat down in the lobby to wait for Molly.

'Do you mind if I join you?' The question was a formality. Even as she asked, the woman who had spoken was easing herself into a deep armchair opposite me; she settled her many shopping bags around her and ordered tea from a passing waitress. This was in the days before the smoking ban, and now she didn't even bother to ask if I had any objection, but took out her cigarettes and lit up. She smoked in a slightly exaggerated fashion. Although she was in late middle age, her pose was that of a young woman who has recently taken up cigarettes in an attempt to appear sophisticated. She was a strange little person, with powdery make-up. I also noticed that she was wearing a lot of costume jewellery, cheap rings with bright fake stones.

'Are you up from the country?' she asked me.

'No, I'm over from London for a few days.'

'I'm here to see my son.'

'Is he staying in the hotel?' I asked.

'No, I mean "here" as in "here in Dublin". I spent this afternoon with him. He isn't well.' As she imparted this last piece of information she stared down at the table-top, sternly implying that this subject was strictly off-limits, which made me wonder why she had mentioned it at all.

'You've been shopping,' I remarked, indicating the carrier bags at her feet, and she brightened at this. She told me that she loved shopping in Dublin; that she didn't get to the city anything like as much as she wanted. She was only here for the day, she was passing time in the hotel waiting for her train home. I asked her where she lived and she pretended she hadn't heard me. Her life, she said, was lonely. She was a widow. 'My husband died many years ago; I'm all alone in the world.'

'At least you have your son,' I reminded her, and she shot back immediately, 'Have you any children?'

'I don't.'

'Well if you did you would know,' she said enigmatically, stubbing out her cigarette as the coffee arrived. And then, most unexpectedly, she gave me a most engaging smile. 'Won't you join me in coffee? Waitress, bring another cup, please.'

There was something so bizarre about the rapport between us that I was beginning to enjoy it. I couldn't figure this woman out at all, with her overstated femininity and her shifting humours, drawing me towards her emotionally and then pushing me away again. I felt that she wanted to confide in me – there was something complicit, conspiratorial about her – but when I responded to this she became haughty and distant. She complimented me extravagantly on my unremarkable clothes. Several of my questions, all seemingly innocuous, she quite simply ignored. I had never before met anyone who behaved as she did, and the playwright in me was fascinated. People actually tend to be predictable in their thought and behaviour; originality is more uncommon than you might imagine. Even when people are bizarre they tend to be so in ways that one has already encountered many times before. My little companion, now full of charm, now latent hostility, was as psychologically strange a person as I had ever come across.

And then Molly arrived. She walked over to where we were sitting and stared at us, from the woman to me and back again, without saying a word. The woman met her stare at first with cold indifference, and then all of a sudden she turned on a smile, a great beaming, delighted smile, and she said, 'Molly! Why look who it is! It's Molly Fox!' This surprised me, for I would never have taken her for a theatre-goer. Let me also at this point put my hands up and admit that I can at times be stupid, stupid beyond belief. Finally Molly spoke. 'What is this? Some kind of conspiracy?' and she glared at me. 'What's going on here?' The nature of the situation was becoming apparent, and I could scarcely believe it. This was one of those incredible coincidences which life occasionally throws up and which one can never replicate in a novel or a play because it would seem unconvincing, a mere device. 'Why, Molly . . .' the woman began in coaxing, emollient tones, at which Molly exploded.

'You're to leave Fergus be. Do you hear me? Stay out of his life.'

'This is ridiculous, I've never heard such nonsense. I'm his mother.'

'Is it not enough that you've driven him mad? Do you want to kill him too?' Molly was shouting at the top of her voice. People in the lobby stopped what they were doing and turned to look at us. Molly was making a scene: shy, self-effacing, timid Molly, who usually slipped in and out of shops and restaurants with her head down, unnoticed and unrecognised.

'The only thing wrong with Fergus is that he won't stand on his own two feet. You won't let him,' Molly's mother said. 'And anyway Fergus wants me to see him. Why do you think I'm here? Who do you think told me he was in hospital again?' Through all of this she was smiling, a small, faintly amused smile.

'Stay away from him,' Molly commanded. 'Stay out of his life.' She nodded to me curtly to pick up my luggage and to follow her, which I meekly did.

It was raining when we left the hotel, and we took a taxi from the rank at the door. We didn't speak much on the journey to her house. I said, 'I hadn't known that Fergus was back in hospital,' and she said, 'Well, he is.' Then she turned and stared sullenly through the wet windscreen at the streets slipping past us. I was taken aback, both at how Molly had behaved in the hotel and how she was behaving now. What had I done wrong? How could I possibly have known the identity of the stranger who had buttonholed me? Hindsight, of course, is a wonderful thing. Now that I knew the connection I could see how there was an odd likeness to Molly that shimmered in her mother. But what had astounded me about what Molly had done earlier was that *she had been acting*.

I need to clarify here what I mean by this. There are some actors who never stop acting. Indeed there are some *people* who never stop acting. Whole societies. There's the old joke about how everyone in Italy is an actor but only the ones who are no good at it take it up professionally. What I'm talking about here are people who work on stage and who use the skills of their profession in their everyday life to distance those around them, to make an illusion, to create the self which they feel any given situation requires. Which is all very well unless the person for whom this is intended rumbles what's happening. Towards the end of our time together, Ken did this increasingly towards me, and I was aware that the bright, teasing person I was encountering wasn't the man with whom I had been planning to spend the rest of my life. It was years before I could see why he was doing it – alarm, I suspect, at the unadorned reality of my own personality. Be that as it may, once you're conscious of what's happening, it's incredibly tiresome.

Actors who habitually do what I'm describing in their daily life come across as exactly what someone who has no knowledge whatsoever of the theatre world would expect an actor to be. Most of these irritating drama queens are not very convincing when they're actually on stage. The very best actors tend to be as Ken was before he started throwing up his smokescreen – quietly complex, understated almost to the point of dullness. One might have been easily convinced that he was spending his life holding down some unexciting desk job in middle-management. And much the same was true of Molly, or had been for me, until this evening.

You're to leave Fergus be! Do you hear me? Stay out of his life. When Molly uttered these words she hadn't been simply talking, she had been delivering lines. This was Molly Fox playing an outraged woman named Molly Fox who was defending her vulnerable brother against the woman who had all but destroyed his life: their own mother. She brought to this role all her skill, all her years of experience on stage. Ostensibly addressing her mother and me, her voice was expertly pitched and modulated to reach everyone who was present in the lobby that day: the astonished waitresses, the bemused guests. She played it like one of the big roles for women, played it with the dark and complex energies required for Lady Macbeth or Hedda Gabler. And I was in the supporting role: ever the stooge, no progress made since my student days as Second Gentlewoman. I was somewhere between sarcasm and genuine admiration when I said to her in the taxi, 'That was quite a performance back there.'

She turned to me with a look of such sincere misery in her brown eyes that I regretted having spoken. I attempted then to apologise but she shook her head and indicated to me not to speak in front of the taxi driver. All I could do was take her hand in mine and to my relief she gripped it tightly. Then she closed her eyes and rested her head against the back of the seat, looking drained and exhausted.

I was deeply unsettled by what had happened. Finally I had met this person who had cast such a shadow over Molly and Fergus's lives. I realised how much thought I too had given to her over the years. Although Molly rarely spoke of her, and then only in the most allusive, elliptical fashion, the idea of her had been constant. Being in her presence, I had experienced that strange sense of parallax I was later to know when meeting David again, almost as if one was encountering two people at the same time. In the case of Molly's mother, even when she was physically present there before me I had been conscious above all of a sense of absence; of a failure, more than that, a refusal to communicate something of herself. I remembered what Louis had said to me not long before we parted, when he was struggling to understand what was happening between us: *You won't let me know you.* Before I met her, Molly's mother had been inconceivable to me. I couldn't conjure up in my mind the woman who had done what Molly said she had done. To think about her had been like trying to imagine God. The banality of her – the powdery make-up, the tacky jewellery – had therefore come as something of a shock; but on reflection it was that withholding of herself, that unfathomable, sly, smiling coolness that seemed more sinister to me than, say, a bad temper or aggressive personality would have been. This woman would not just deny responsibility for any problem, she would look at you, detached, amused, and deny that any problem existed.

The taxi was stifling. The driver had the heat turned up full-blast against the raw chill of the night, and there was a smell of artificial coconut, some kind of air-freshener that was supposed to sweeten the atmosphere but was actually most unpleasant. I squeezed Molly's hand tightly and gave precise directions to the driver as we drew near to the house. I paid him and we got out of the car, stood for a moment on the pavement with my bags while the taxi turned and drove off. Molly stared at her own dark house, at the dripping garden with its lank plants, and then she said to me, 'I can only cope with her by being false. What sort of a relationship is that?' I put my case down in a puddle and took her in my arms. She was stiff and resistant, but I held her all the same.

It was strange to remember all this now. It made me shiver, in spite of the heat of summer. As I drew near to the house I noticed a man walking a short distance ahead of me, and to my surprise he turned in at Molly's place. He closed the gate precisely behind him, and I had to push it open again with my hip. He was ringing the door-bell as I walked up the path; he heard my footsteps and turned around. I recognised him immediately, even though it was years since we had met.

'Hello, Fergus.' He stared at me in dismay. He recognised me too, uttered my name aloud as though it were the most disappointing word possible in any language. And then he said, 'I don't believe this. I'm so stupid. Molly told me. Molly told me and I forgot. She said she was going to New York and that you'd be staying here. I'm stupid, stupid, stupid.' Fumbling for the keys, I told him not to worry, it was a happy accident; I was glad to have the company, as I was a bit lonely here on my own. I said this out of politeness but realised as I spoke that it was actually true. Would he not come in for a few moments? It was all I could do to persuade him, but he was confused and despondent, and that made him more tractable. As he stepped into the hall the long-case clock struck four with its deep, soft chime. I closed the front door, and suddenly he seemed to relax a little, as the peace and beauty of Molly's house enfolded us.

I led him down to the kitchen and dumped my bags of shopping on the table. Unfortunately there was an opened bottle of wine on the counter, only a glass or so of it gone. While Fergus isn't an alcoholic, drink has periodically been one of the problems in his life. 'What can I get you, Fergus? What would you like?' I saw him looking at the bottle. I moved ever so slightly to the left, so as to block it from his view, and gave him what I hoped was an engaging smile. 'Coffee? Tea?'

'I'll tell you what I'd love. I'd love a drink.' I said nothing, but I kept smiling at him. 'I'd love a drink of water. Big glass. Nice and cold.' I realised then that he'd been teasing me, he'd known what I'd been thinking.

'That's all? Nothing else?'

'Could we sit in the garden?' he said timidly. 'I'd like a cigarette, and Molly doesn't let me smoke in the house.'

I unlocked the back door, and he went outside while I filled a jug at the kitchen sink. As I was adding some ice cubes I could see him wandering about on the grass. By the time I joined him in the garden, he was sitting on a bench looking at the ground and dragging on a cigarette.

'Thanks awfully. It's a hot day.' I agreed and for a few moments we made small talk about the weather, about the solstice, about heat and light. He looked very like Molly, but Molly at her most nondescript, Molly as she was when she didn't want to be recognised and refused to project her personality. Fergus was incapable of that transformation that could make his sister such an electrifying presence on stage, and indeed in her private life, when she so desired. He was a small man, lightly built, with brown hair and the same olive complexion as Molly. He reminded me of nothing so much as a little wild bird, a sparrow or a dunnock, and in dealing with him I always felt I had to behave as if he were indeed such a creature. Anything sudden or abrupt would startle him; he needed stillness and calm. He took out a packet of cigarettes and lit a new one off the stub of the one he had just finished. 'Isn't the cow dreadful?' he remarked unexpectedly, indicating it with a toss of his head. 'I said to Molly, "What possessed you? It ruins the whole garden." But she just laughed.'

I forgot to mention the voice. Like his sister, Fergus is blessed with a magically beautiful voice. Deep and nuanced, it has that same breaking quality in moments of emotion that makes Molly's voice so affecting; it gives weight and resonance to his most inconsequential remarks. When she talks to me about his life and how things haven't worked out for him, his voice is something that she comes back to again and again. *I know actors who would sell their own grandmothers for a voice like that.* I think that it would pain her to see any such gift not being used to its full effect, never mind the grief for her brother that is implicated in this particular case. He is also a very fine singer. Once, Molly was appearing in a play that called for an unaccompanied male voice to be heard singing a verse of a hymn offstage. She managed to coax Fergus into making a tape, which she then played for the director, who listened to it simply to humour her, but was won over immediately. And so it came to pass that it was Fergus's voice that was heard as Molly stood alone and immobile in a pool of light that slowly faded to blackness as the singing ended. It was a thrilling moment, but Fergus never got to experience it himself. By the time the play went up his life had gone into a serious tailspin, yet again, and for several months he was once more incapacitated. I was never sure that it wasn't his involvement in the play that had actually provoked the crisis, but I never said that to Molly.

He was still smoking and gazing out over the garden. 'I told her she should have got a dog rather than a fake cow. A real dog, I mean.'

'She's away a lot. It's impossible to look after a dog properly when you're all over the place the way Molly is.'

'That's what she said, but I told her I'd look after it. I'd mind it at my place, or I'd come over here every day if she preferred. Feed it. Take it for walks. I know she was tempted. She likes dogs.'

'She does,' I agreed.

'We always had dogs when we were children,' Fergus said. 'We had a spaniel called Bingo. Gorgeous creature, she was, so gentle. Sort of toffee-coloured. I still remember the feel of her ears, like silk they were . . .' His voice trailed away.

'Why "Bingo"?'

'Do you know, I have absolutely no idea. I can't remember now.' Unusually, he looked me straight in the eye as he said this, and he smiled. I was the one who glanced away, overwhelmed by the combination of the lost child in him with his memories, and that haunting voice. How did Molly bear it? I picked up my glass and drank some of the icy cold water.

'Are you writing a new play?' he asked me shyly, and I said that I was attempting to do so. 'Will there be a part in it for Molly?'

'I'm not sure yet. It would be good if it turned out that

way. I'd love to work with her again. But it's early days yet. All I know is that it's about a hare.' He stared at me, astonished, and then I realised that he'd misunderstood. 'That's H-A-R-E,' I added, and we both laughed.

'You had me worried there for a minute. And how does the hare fit in? Is it a character? Will you have a real live animal there on the stage?'

'I don't know. I'm still playing about with the idea, I haven't actually started writing it yet.' I don't usually talk to people about work in progress; that I did so today was a sign of my desperation. I had hoped that spoken of aloud it would impress me too, but that trick hadn't worked.

'Molly's going to London after New York, isn't she?' he said. 'She's making one of those book things, tapes that people listen to in the car. I've got all of them. *The Mayor of Casterbridge. Wuthering Heights. Jane Eyre.* She's amazing on that one. *There was no possibility of taking a walk that day.* I listen to them at night when I can't get to sleep.'

I take back any impression I may have given that Fergus lacks his sister's charisma. He may not have her ability to transform herself, to project dramatically, but his quiet charms are powerfully beguiling. The intimate and confiding manner, together with his gentleness, his sweet nature, is quite a combination. If he knew what he was about you'd call him the most subtle of seducers. That he doesn't know – and he really doesn't – almost beggars belief. This lack of self-knowledge, and its consequences, exasperates Molly no end.

'This is how it works,' she'd explained to me once. 'Fergus meets a woman. He reels her in without even trying. She thinks he's the sweetest, kindest man she's ever met, and he may well be. Fergus thinks that at last he's found what he's wanted all his life, someone who loves him. He doesn't pick up on the fact that she doesn't know him. For a while things bowl along well enough, and Fergus thinks he's happy. And then it begins to unravel. Women pay a lot of lip service to the idea of romantic love, but it's all nonsense. They're generally looking for money and security, for social power.' I protested the cynicism of this. 'Maybe you're right,' she replied ironically. 'Maybe there are plenty of women out there who'd be happy to share their life with one of the most endearing men you could ever meet, who'd overlook the problems he has through no fault of his own, but wherever these women are, Fergus never seems to meet them.'

She was being disingenuous and she knew it. Fergus's problems were no small thing, and fretting about them had blighted Molly's own life for years. The heavy drinking and the bouts of depression, the serious medication and the inability to have a real career, his general helplessness and haplessness: you would have had to wonder about the woman who would have willingly chosen to take all of this on board and engage with it. I said as much to Molly.

'But *I* engage with it!' she said with sudden passion. 'I love Fergus and I'll never let him down.' I backed off at that point. Close as I was to Molly, the conversation was moving into a place where I had no business being and didn't want to go. I looked at Fergus sitting beside me, quietly smoking his cigarette. Heartbreaking, it must be, to have such a brother. Suddenly I felt that if I were Molly, I might well have cut Fergus out of my life. I

knew she'd thought of it occasionally. There were periods when she distanced herself from him, when he was
well enough to be left to get on with his life while she got
on with hers. But there were also crises time and time
again that wore her down emotionally and mentally. She
told me of a recurrent nightmare she had, crudely simple
in its psychology but none the less powerful for that,
none the less terrifying, of trying to save Fergus from
drowning and realising that they were both going to go
under. Terrifying, yes, that's what he was, this gentle,
broken man who sat before me in the scented summer
garden, drinking iced water and making banal conversation. At this precise moment I couldn't imagine a more
unnerving sibling. To look at him and to see yourself, the
same physique, the same rare gift, and to see what had
become of him, and to know that it could so easily have
happened to you. Molly was heroic, saintly, I thought.
Her circumstances would have defeated most people:
they would certainly have defeated me. Fergus was a
dangerous man, with his tenderness and his charm and
the deep and unending darkness of his mind that was an
abyss into which Molly might also vanish one day if she
wasn't strong enough. There was no knowing when, if
ever, she might reach tipping point. He repelled me even
as my heart went out to him for all he had suffered and
lost.

'Do you know what she's doing in New York?' I asked
him.

'It's just a holiday, as far as I'm aware. You know
Molly. She loves cities and the bigger the better. She likes
to be alone while knowing that there are lots of people
around her.'

'That's true,' I agreed, remembering the first time I ever saw Molly, sitting reading her book in a café, with that great rope of dark hair draped over her shoulder.

'She seems to be having a great time,' Fergus went on. 'She's got a ticket for the opera for tonight.'

'You've spoken to her recently?'

'She called me yesterday. It wouldn't be possible for Molly to go more than a couple of days without speaking to me.' I was struck by the unconscious egotism of this, and he noticed me noticing. My unspoken objection to what he had said hung in the air between us. It seemed to amuse him faintly, for he gave a little smile but said nothing. After a moment or two, to break a silence that was becoming increasingly awkward, I asked him, 'How's your job going these days?'

'Oh, much as ever. It's incredibly boring, just basic office stuff, but at least it's a job. They're very understanding when I'm stretchered off, and that counts for a lot.'

'Architect's office, isn't it?'

'No, a solicitor's. I had to leave the architect's a few years back. The boss was so aggressive; I just couldn't take it. *Fergus, you did this. Fergus, you did that.* Always shouting at me. I hate aggressive people. It was a pity because the job itself was more interesting than where I am now.' I saw in his eyes a flash of that vulnerability and fear I always expected to find in him; and I realised that it had been strikingly absent today, up until this moment. He drew hard on his cigarette. 'The solicitor's is all right, they're decent to me. I'm lucky to have work. And I like the place where I'm living. I can walk into town in twenty minutes, and it's on a direct bus route to here, so it's handy for when I want to come and see Molly.

Obviously it's nothing like this,' and he gestured towards the garden, the house. 'It's a flat and it's small, but it gets a lot of light and the landlord's nice. I was lucky to find it.'

I've always liked Fergus, even though I've never got to know him very well. Pretty well all our meetings have taken place by chance here in Molly's house, with months or even sometimes years between them. She would never have willingly brought us into each other's company, much less fostered strong links between us, and it occurred to me that this was yet another area where things weren't quite on the level with her. It was all very well for her to befriend my brother, for Tom to become her spiritual guide and mentor, but it would have been quite another thing for Fergus and me to have any sort of friendship independent of Molly.

After I split up with Louis I took my broken heart to Dublin, to Molly's house. Much to my embarrassment Fergus happened to call round and was witness to my tears, my red eyes and swollen face. 'I hate you seeing me like this,' I said, sniffing and gulping, to which he replied, 'Oh come now, it shouldn't bother you at all, given the way you've seen me over the years.' That pulled me up short. I had known Fergus anaesthetised by drink. I had seen him curled up in a blanket on Molly's sofa, speechless with grief, like a man who was turning into stone. I had briefly seen him on one of the several occasions when he was hospitalised for depression, when Molly hadn't been able to face going into the ward on her own; and to my shame I had never realised how humiliating Fergus might find all of this in his more lucid and coherent hours.

The cat that had pestered me at lunchtime was back in the garden now. Fergus stubbed out his cigarette and coaxed it over to him, set it on his lap and petted it. The creature settled down there and let him make quite free with it. He had turned up one of its paws and was studying the soft pink pads when he suddenly asked me a question completely out of left field: 'Have you ever met my mother?'

'No Fergus, I haven't.'

This was an instinctive lie rather than a calculated one, and I regretted it immediately. Perhaps Fergus was being disingenuous: perhaps Molly had told him about our encounter with their mother and he was curious to hear my version of what had taken place. If this was the case he was being most duplicitous, for he released the cat's paw and took to stroking its head, and said, 'No, I don't suppose you would ever have had occasion to meet, now I come to think of it.'

'What's she like?' I dared to ask.

'Mummy?' He considered this for a few moments and then he said, 'Remote. She's a nice person but she's hard to get to know. She doesn't like people to get close to her emotionally. You can get to a certain point and then she draws back, becomes distant, and that can be hard to take. But it's just the way she is,' he said mildly. 'Everybody has their own peculiarities, don't they?' They most certainly do, I thought. 'I actually think they're quite alike, Mummy and Molly, but Molly hates me saying that. It's true though, isn't it? Molly's the best in the world and I don't know how I'd have got this far in life without her, but she's remote in that same way. She doesn't like anybody to get too close.' I asked him if he saw his mother often.

'I try to. It isn't always easy. She doesn't live in Dublin

and neither of us can drive, so it's awkward. I worry a lot about her, now that she's getting older. I think she's lonely. There's not much I can do but I hate to think of her being isolated.' He lifted his gaze from the cat on his knee and looked me straight in the eye. 'Do you think there's any way you could persuade Molly to make her peace with our mother? Molly likes you lots. She's as close to you as she is to anyone. She might listen.' Given the way the conversation was developing, I thought it best to be straight with him.

'Fergus,' I said, 'that's a pretty tall order. She's extremely hostile to your mother.'

'Oh, she can't stand her. Molly *hates* Mummy, I'm fully aware of that. She can't tolerate being in the same room. She blames our mother for everything, especially for all my troubles.'

'And you don't?'

'Of course not.' He was still holding my gaze with unusual firmness of purpose for such a shy man. 'My life is a shambles. No, let's not pretend otherwise,' for he saw me begin to demur. 'A total shambles. I don't have any of the things a man in his mid-thirties might reasonably expect to have – a home of his own, a wife or a partner, maybe children, a career. And I mean a career, not a job: not a dazzling career like Molly's, I know how rare that is, but not a dead-end lousy clerking job either, like the one I'm stuck in. I'm aware how little all of what I have amounts to; and when I wake in the small hours and think about it, it's more unimpressive still, believe me. But here's the key point,' and he laid his hand over his heart. 'My life is *my life*. Not my mother's or Molly's or anyone else's but *mine*. And I take full responsibility for it.

Wouldn't that be the worst thing of all? To be a man of thirty-five and still be blaming one's mother for life not having worked out as one might have wanted it to?' He paused for a moment to let me consider this idea.

'Do you ever talk to Molly about this?'

'Are you kidding? It's off the agenda. Mummy's a monster, and everything's her fault. End of story. Nothing to discuss. Why do you think I'm talking to you?'

'And have you spoken to your mother?'

'We have discussed it at length over the years, but there's nothing much more to be said now. I try to avoid the subject. I don't like to upset her. In any case, what I'm telling you is that it's Molly's perspective that's wrongheaded and causing problems, not my mother's.'

'Fergus,' I said, 'everything you're telling me is so much at odds with what I thought was the situation in your family that I'm at a loss to know what to say.'

'I know,' he replied, and he sighed. 'I can well imagine all this must come as a shock, and I'm sorry to spring it on you so suddenly. But I must admit that I'm glad to be having this conversation. I think it was meant to be. In all the years you and Molly have known each other, this is the first time we've met without her also being present. Isn't that strange?'

'Did you plan this? Am I being set up?'

'Oh no, no, far from it.' I considered this for a moment: I believed him. He broke my gaze and looked away down the long scented garden, at the fruit bushes and the roses before he turned to me again.

He told me that he thought his mother should never have married. It wasn't that she made a bad marriage, it was that she was unsuited to the whole state of married life. 'She had been brought up in a generation where it was what was expected of a woman, and so a great many married and had children, whether it suited them or not. At least my mother had the self-knowledge to realise what she had done, and you have to give her credit for that. I think a lot of women were in the same position but they couldn't see the damage they were doing. By the time she understood the situation, it was too late, in that Molly and I had arrived on the scene. So I think that the whole time we were small she was wondering should she stay or should she go – which would do least harm.'

'Whereas Molly's view is that she just got fed up with the situation and shipped out.'

'Exactly.'

I felt that the man with whom I was having this conversation was not the person with whom I had sat down about half an hour earlier. For me that Fergus – timid, weak, a failure in life – had disappeared for ever. This new Fergus was a man of wisdom and acute moral knowledge. He had had the courage and insight to inspect his own life more closely than most might dare to do, and he had compassion and forgiveness for those who had hurt him. The memory of that detached, coolly amused woman whom I had briefly met tempered my thoughts: I might have considered him less extraordinary had I not seen what he was up against, although it was imperative now that he should never know I'd met her. It didn't matter that his life, in social terms, was not a success. To expect someone to gain a mature perspective on their troubled life as he had, and to also expect them to have worked out to their advantage all those other things such as property, relationships and career that we mistakenly confuse with life itself – that would have been unreasonable. What he had achieved seemed to me more precious by far.

'There's no villain in all of this,' he said. 'Mummy didn't deliberately set out to cause harm, any more than I intended all the grief and trouble I've given Molly over the years.' Molly. I'd thought she had won through in life, whilst Fergus was defeated, broken. Now it seemed to me that things were perhaps quite the opposite, and her brother's woes notwithstanding, Molly was the one who really hadn't come to terms with the past, who was still bitter about it in a way that was corrosive and did more harm to her than to anyone else. I felt that Molly herself knew this. What else was her connection with Tom but an attempt to find that understanding, that forgiveness that her brother had come to? And if Tom hadn't got her there, what hope was there for me?

'Maybe someday I'll talk to Molly about this as you ask. The one thing I can't promise is that it'll make any difference.'

'Don't underestimate all the trouble I've had, but don't make the mistake either of disregarding all that she's achieved. Molly Fox: she's remarkable. You do know that today's her birthday?'

'I do.' I felt a sudden anger for Molly's sake. 'You can say what you want about your mother, she certainly picked her moment.'

'I think these moments pick themselves, don't you? When something's over, it's over. You know yourself, I suppose, when a relationship's run its course you can't simply string it along for a week or so more just because Christmas, say, is coming or somebody's birthday. I think that's how Mummy would reason it.'

Now I didn't know what I thought. Perhaps Molly was right, and her poisonous mother had turned Fergus's head, justifying her own actions to make herself feel better. Of course you could hang on for extra time. Some people lived a lie their whole lives, and was that worse than abandoning two small children? Anyway, it was done now, and it had been a disaster.

'I used to think I remembered this day,' he said. 'I mean Molly's seventh birthday, the day my mother left. I can see the two of us eating ice creams, and I'm crying. But then someone told me that if you can see yourself in a memory, as if you're watching a film, then it isn't true. And I'm afraid that's how it is in this particular instance. I can see two small children, one of whom is me, in our kitchen at home. But maybe my father or Molly told me that one time, that we had ice creams and I cried, and I'm imagining that I remember it.'

He moved to take something from his pocket, and in doing so he accidentally dislodged the cat. He winced as it hooked its claws into his leg to try to prevent itself from slipping off his lap, but the pain made him push it away. The cat tumbled to the grass almost in slow motion and slunk off down the garden, disgruntled. I had thought Fergus was looking for his cigarettes, but instead from his jacket he took a small wooden box. 'I bought this for Molly. It's a little present for her birthday. You know she doesn't really celebrate it. I'm the only person she accepts presents from today.' He couldn't keep a childlike note of pride out of his voice as he said this.

The box was made of contrasting pale and dark woods, and one narrow side had been fashioned to resemble the spine of a book. But it was hinged, and when Fergus released a metal clasp on the other side of the box it opened out flat. I saw then that it contained a miniature chess set. The board and the chess men were also made of the same contrasting woods. There were holes in the board, and each of the tiny chess pieces, intricately carved, was fitted with a peg on the bottom, by which it could be slotted into the holes. Fergus moved a few pieces across the board at random to show me how it functioned. I wished that I had chanced upon it in a shop so that it could have been my gift to Molly, because I could think of few things that would have appealed to her more. Everything about it – its small scale, its concealment and intricacy – would delight her.

'Do you think she'll like it?' Again that voice, so mellifluous, so haunting.

'I do, Fergus. I think she'll like it very much.' He placed it on the table for me to give to her on her return, and stood up. 'I should be going now.'

He followed me out of the garden and back into the house. We fell again to small talk, as we had done on his arrival. I regretted that he had wanted no more than cold water to drink; he wished me well for my play. We both hoped to meet again before long. He stopped in the hall before all Molly's photos, her trophies and prizes and posters, and we stood there together for a moment looking at them. There were pictures of Molly in full Restoration costume, as a flapper, in a draped Greek garment; pictures of her alone, of her locked in an embrace with someone, of her laughing. In all of them she was striking. Even in stills she conveyed the energy she transmitted on stage. 'She was so young then,' Fergus remarked, pointing at one of the photographs. 'Look how long her hair was.'

'That was the first time we worked together. That was my play, *Summer with Lucy*.' I didn't say it to him but it seemed like a lifetime ago now. He then inspected the trophies while I inspected him. 'I know this must sound odd, but sometimes, even yet, I can hardly believe that she's my sister. When I see her like this, professionally, I mean, and I think of how much she's achieved . . . I suppose I realise I don't tell her often enough how much I admire her.'

'I'm sure she knows, Fergus.' He raised his eyes and looked at me. I knew then how hard it would be for me to find a way to express my admiration for him. I knew he would never believe me.

The clock chimed again as Fergus left. He had been there for an hour; it was later than I had thought. When I went back down to the kitchen I was struck by how it had changed since the morning, with the changing light of the day. I had seen this room – and this house – at all seasons, at all times of the day and night. I had been here when the whole place was cocooned with snow. I had seen it by candlelight. I had been here during heavy rain, the kind of rain that becomes pleasurable to watch because it makes of the house a haven. The rooms in which one moves become a world apart from the wet streets, the sodden garden. The kitchen now had moved into shadow; it had become a more sombre place than it had been this morning. The things I had bought in town were still sitting on the kitchen table where I had dumped them on Fergus's arrival, and I had just about time to tidy them away. The second part of Andrew's series on memorials would be starting on television shortly, and I wanted to see it.

When I switched on, the opening credits were already

running, a flowing sequence of images, stained glass, paintings and cathedral facades that faded into each other and was overlain by staccato minimalist music. When the actual programme began, the opening shot was of Andrew standing before the Menin Gate. The camera pulled back from him to reveal how vast the structure was, and then panned over the lists and lists of the war dead. 'What do we intend,' he asked in a voice-over, 'when we memorialise? Is it simply to do honour, and if so to what? To the person or to our memory of the person? Is it that we want someone not to be forgotten? And is that genuinely possible? Is not our wish to, quite literally, set in stone, our thoughts and feelings, our memories and our idea of someone who is now dead – is not that wish in its very essence a futile one?'

To begin with, he concentrated on the difference between public and private memorialising. He went from the Menin Gate to a huge cemetery from the First World War, inspecting individual graves as people tended to them, placing flowers and flags. He contrasted this with the tomb of the Unknown Soldier in Westminster Abbey and with a tiny war memorial in a Cotswold village. In everything he said he operated at the highest levels of intellectual debate, but there was such clarity to his thought, such logic and a kind of exalted simplicity to his ideas, that what he was saying was made accessible to pretty well anyone who might care to listen. There was also an enormous sympathy in his presentation, an emotional undertow that tempered the scholarly and subtly emphasised the deep humanity of the subject. There is something about Andrew that he can only communicate when he is in front of a camera. Even though he is an outstanding teacher and lecturer, he only really comes into his own when he is being filmed. The impersonality of the medium allows that extra degree of emotional privacy into which he can relax, so that each viewer feels he is speaking directly to them, and to them alone. He conveys a sense of intimacy that is beyond what he ever makes available in his private life. That and his remarkable capacity for intellectual synthesis are at the core of his success.

He talked about how, with the decline of religious belief, our concept of death changed in society as a whole. More than that, he quoted Virginia Woolf's remark about how sometime around 1910 human nature changed, and argued convincingly that this was more germane to the issue of memorialising than anything to do with religion. 'It is our attitude to life that is ultimately more significant than our attitude to death.' Time and again he came back to this idea of the self, of what had brought about this change in perception (the development of psychology, the wars of the twentieth century, the rise of science and rationalism). The self we were left with after all this was, according to Andrew, a much more nebulous and evanescent thing, more socially determined than would have been conceivable in the nineteenth century.

He used an exhibition of quilts commemorating people who had died of AIDS to illustrate what he was saying and to show how the nature of memorials had to change as a result of these changed perceptions. Quilting had always been considered a folk tradition rather than an art form. It was an area of female activity, unlike stone cutting or wood carving, the products of which were more enduring and therefore had always been seen as more suitable for memorials. 'For the one thing we always wanted to believe about such constructions – tombs, statues, monuments – was that they were built to last. Unlike the things they represented, they would *endure*.' Cue to weathered headless angels in a Victorian cemetery, full of broken statuary. While the AIDS quilts were undoubtedly a continuation of a certain tradition, they also indicated a radical break with the past, 'a new kind of memorial for a new idea of the self'.

Walking amongst the coloured quilts, with their embroidered names, dates and symbols of flowers, rainbows, notes of music and so on, he remarked on their aesthetic, simply on how attractive they were as objects. 'And that, I must admit, is something that has often given me problems about certain memorials,' Andrew confessed to the camera. 'The discrepancy there is between the undeniable beauty of the memorial itself and the ugliness, the terrible violence of the deaths they record: acts of war, acts of the utmost inhumanity.'

The scene moved to Paris, to Île de la Cité, with Notre Dame behind him. 'I'm here to visit not the cathedral,' he said, 'but the memorial to the some 200,000 people deported from France during World War Two, amongst them Jewish people, resistance workers and forced labourers.' He descended a flight of steps and was confronted by black iron bars and spikes. 'Already there is a sense of narrowness and constriction.' He turned and as he entered a doorway, said: 'It's difficult for us to film here. This is a dark place. It's cramped and claustrophobic, intentionally so; and even on a hot afternoon such as we have today, one is chilled.' In a low voice he described the interlinked cell-like structures, the metal bars, the thousands of tiny lights and the single bare bulb, the poems on the walls, the names of the camps to which the deported had been sent. 'This is a profoundly moving place. There is also something terrible and desolate about it. It is not a place to which one would wish to return, but it is a place which stays in the mind and in the heart long after one has been here. I realise that our filming today is to a large degree inadequate, but I make no apology for it. This is not a place you see. This is a place you experience.' I expected the camera to move to another place at that point, to another stele or plaque. Instead, it cropped closely to Andrew's face.

'But harrowing as this place is,' he said, 'I think that I would argue in favour of something more extreme still. There is a certain aesthetic at work here. Some crimes are so ugly, such an affront to humanity, that only a brutal, raw, even crude response is adequate. Anything else seems dishonest and disrespectful.'

Now he was in a garden, a strange garden that was full of dark vegetation, hellebores and low plants with sharply pointed black leaves. 'But who after all are memorials for?' Andrew asked as he walked slowly towards a bench and sat down. 'Are they for the living or the dead? By their very beauty can they offer comfort to those who have suffered loss, those who are left behind? Surely the answer must be yes. Surely this is one of the most important functions of a memorial, to redeem suffering through beauty.'

In the closing sequences he drew together the various strands of thought he had explored in the course of the programme. The final shot found him walking through a cornfield, full of bright poppies. 'I'm back where I started.

The Menin Gate is a few kilometres west of here. That massive stone monument is a thing of its time. We live in a more vertiginous age, an age of doubt and reason. There's something almost weightless about our world, I think, something fleeting and insubstantial that's ill at ease with any pretence of certainty.' The camera moved in for a close-up of a poppy moving in the wind, with its crumpled red petals and black heart. 'There can be no more fitting memorial to the Great War, when a whole world passed away, than these poppies: than the fields of Flanders themselves.' At that the camera pulled back to show thousands upon thousands of poppies scattered through the cornfield that stretched to the far horizon.

'Well, you've changed your tune,' I thought to myself as the final credits rolled and I remembered how dismissive he'd been of a Dublin sky all those years ago in college. Nothing would have been good enough for him then but art of the highest order. A week ago I had seen the first programme in the series, in which he'd dealt with the ancient world, with Greece, Rome and Etruria. He'd remarked upon how sometimes it was tempting to disregard what one knew of the function or meaning of some of the objects concerned, tomb paintings and marble steles, and to consider them purely in aesthetic terms, to project upon them our own feelings and ideas. When we looked at a terracotta sarcophagus on which sat life-sized figures of a man and a woman it was difficult not to interpret it in the light of our own conception of what the relations between a couple might be; to bring to bear upon it sentimental feelings that would have been incomprehensible to the Etruscans themselves. One of the most difficult things of all, he had said, was to stand outside our own time, to see the society in which we lived with a similar distance and detachment. Even to attempt to do it brought great insight. In tonight's programme I had sensed a kind of unease, as if he himself was not fully convinced of the arguments he was making.

I switched off the television and went down to the kitchen. I cooked the fish I had bought earlier, watching under the eye-level grill as the flesh became white and opaque. I put together a simple salad and cut bread. All the time I was preparing this meal and then eating it at the kitchen table I was thinking about Fergus. How completely I had bought Molly's version of him! And even more to the point, how completely I had bought Molly's version of herself. I should have been aware long before now that there was much more to Fergus than the trouble there had been in his life. His distress lay over him like a grey veil, obscuring who and what he was, but not changing his essential self. I could now see his personality and his disturbance as two quite distinct things: connected, yes, but not integral to each other in the way I had thought. This confusion had done him a great disservice. I wished it could be possible for me to develop a friendship with this kind, gentle, witty man, independent of my relationship with his sister, but I knew there was no chance of that.

I felt that I was being disloyal thinking along these lines while I was staying in Molly's place. The sense of it being her house, indeed a sense of Molly herself began to close in around me in the kitchen as it had done, more agreeably, on my waking that morning in the bedroom. On the kitchen table was a willow basket she used as a fruit bowl. There was a blue-and-white china tub for utensils near the sink, bristling with salad servers and wooden spoons; and beside it was an iron trivet in the shape of a flower, to support hot dishes and pans. Looking at these things made me feel weirdly nervous, too close to Molly at a moment when I felt disconnected from her. Beyond the kitchen window I could see the fake cow, that wretched thing that I wouldn't have tolerated in my own life or home for a moment. Now it seemed to me like the most ridiculous affectation, the caprice of a woman with more money than either taste or sense, and I felt a sudden anger within me.

Just at that, the doorbell rang. It startled me but I was glad to hear it because I needed company. I was spiralling into some strange mental state that I only half understood but that I knew I needed to get out of fast. Even if it was only someone selling raffle tickets or looking for directions it would be enough. It would oblige me to put on my social mask for a moment and connect me with another person, and that was what I needed right now.

When I opened the door the caller was standing with his back to me, but I recognised him for all that, and this gave me the upper hand when he turned to face me.

'Hello, Andrew.'

'Molly,' he said. 'Where's Molly?'

'New York.'

'New York?' He could hardly have been more surprised if I'd said that she'd gone to the moon. 'What are you doing here? And what's she doing there?'

'Aren't you going to say hello to me?' He gave an embarrassed little laugh then, apologised and greeted me.

As he bent down and kissed me I remembered something that I neglected to mention earlier: Andrew and I had been to bed together. It only happened once, at the very end of that day I described, the last he spent in Ireland. I had offered him the choice of my absent friends' rooms, but in fact he had spent his second and final night in the house with me. I remembered it now but only the cool fact of it, as one might recall that one had once visited Japan or been far out in a small boat on the open sea without recalling the precise details, without remembering in the fullest sense of the word. I am aware that what I am saying here doesn't tally with what I said to Molly when she asked about this, but that's easily explained: I was lying. It was none of her business. Anyone who asks such a question deserves to be lied to.

'It's Molly's birthday.'

'I know,' I replied to him.

'I hadn't known it was today. I saw it in the paper.'

'I saw it too. She won't be pleased.'

Why is that?'

'Come through to the kitchen,' I said. He was in the hall by now, and I closed the front door behind him.

He looked well, but then he always does. He was dressed in pale clothes and was carrying a soft, biscuit-coloured jacket over his arm. Since he started working on television he has taken on even more of a gloss. People whom one has only known from seeing them on the small screen often look hyper-real in the flesh, and I had always put that down to the difference between the medium and real life. But since Andrew's change of career I've begun to realise that it has more to do with certain habits of dress or grooming, of professional polish, that are required for the cameras and that are then carried on into daily practice.

On returning to the kitchen I was conscious that the air was heavy with the smell of fish, as I hadn't been while I was cooking and eating. I quickly opened the window and moved my dirty plates from the table to the sink. Andrew draped his jacket over the back of a chair and looked suddenly forlorn. I noticed now that he was carrying a paper carrier bag that clearly contained a bottle of champagne and a large book. 'I don't know what to do,' he said. 'I feel like a bit of an idiot.'

'If that champagne is cold we'll drink it now,' I said robustly. 'I'll put a replacement bottle in the fridge for Molly before I leave. I'm absolutely delighted to see you again.'

My suggestion was born out of an attempt to make the best of the situation. Simply by being there I had found out about his plan for a little celebration with Molly, something I suspect he would have preferred me not to know about. Then again, had she been at home, I very much doubt that it would have been the delightful occasion he imagined. All I had to offer him was the red wine sitting on the counter that I had subtly denied Fergus. Cheap plonk with me instead of champagne with Molly: I could well understand Andrew's disappointment. The least I could do was open the bottle.

'It is cold,' he admitted.

'So much the better. We'll take it into the back garden and we'll drink to Molly and to you too. I've just been watching your memorials programme. Congratulations, it was great, really moving.'

'You're very kind to say so. I brought Molly a copy of the book of the series. You'll get your copy when you go back home, I posted it to your house in London the other day.' I thanked him, and he passed me Molly's copy to look at. 'That's the reason I'm in Dublin, to do a few interviews and promotion around the series. I was doing a signing session in a shop in town this afternoon.'

The title of the book showed a photograph of the words 'Remember Me' carved in stone. It was a most impressive volume, with many coloured plates of all kinds of monuments and artworks, and a series of essays. I noticed that the printed dedication at the front read 'i.m. William (Billy) Forde', followed by Billy's dates. 'You're listed in the acknowledgements,' Andrew said.

'Me? But why? What did I do?'

'More than you can ever know. You're my friend and you've always been there for me.' I was taken aback by this frank declaration, and I hardly knew how to reply to Andrew, except to thank him again.

'Anyway, Molly,' he said briskly.' What's she doing in New York?'

'I don't know. I think she's just there for a holiday.'

'On her own? Won't that be terribly lonely?'

'I wouldn't have thought so, not for a lone wolf like Molly.'

'I spoke to her quite recently and she didn't mention it.' I started to explain that she would be there for a week and then was off to London, but he interrupted me. '*Adam Bede*, yes, I know. She did tell me about that. Maybe the States was a last-minute decision.'

'Maybe,' I said, but I knew it hadn't been. She had told me months earlier that she would be away mid-June into July, New York for a week and then London; the house would be available if I wanted it. 'You'd have to talk to Molly herself about all this.'

I started to prepare things for the champagne and asked Andrew to move so that I could get some ice from the fridge. Crossing to the window he glanced out and did the usual double-take with the cow, but realised almost immediately that it wasn't real. 'Fibreglass,' I said helpfully.

'Isn't that just typical of Molly,' he said and he started to laugh.

'Isn't it just,' I said, and the ice cubes rattled into the ice bucket. I had decided to take the line of least resistance as far as Andrew and Molly were concerned. 'Do you like it?'

'It's hilarious. I think it's great.'

I suggested then that he might go out into the garden and wait there while I finished preparing the tray. Andrew likes everything just so, and therefore I hunted down the correct glasses, a white cloth for the tray and another to drape over the bottle. I knew that Molly had such things, and as I searched them out in the drawers and cupboards I glanced out of the window from time to time, keeping an eye on Andrew. It amused me to see him wandering around admiring the flowers, for a more urban man than he, a bigger library cormorant and creature of the great indoors, would be hard to imagine. He studied the bird feeder as though trying to work out what purpose this mysterious object might serve; broke a few spines from a rosemary bush and rubbed them between his fingers, sniffed them with extreme caution, as though fearing their fragrance might knock him unconscious. I finished my preparations just as he was settling down at the table and I carried the tray out to join him.

I got Andrew to open the bottle. He hauled it dripping

from the chrome bucket; it was like an icy baby being born. But he opened it with less style than I had expected, for the cork shot off into a rosebush and some of the champagne gushed out before he could put a tilted glass beneath the neck of the bottle.

'To Molly.'

'To Molly. And to you too, Andrew. "Remember Me".'

The champagne was fragrant, bone-dry, almost metallic but pleasantly so. I said to Andrew that too often any champagne I drank was in a work context, at first nights or press receptions, and it was good to be sharing a bottle with a friend for a change. I was glad to see him. It was about two months since we had last met, but there was nothing unusual in that, given how busy both our lives were.

'And how is the work going at the moment, if I might ask? Are you working on a new play?' When I said that I was he asked me if I felt able to say what it was about. I replied as I had to Fergus, that I hardly knew myself because it was still at such an early stage. I sat quietly for a moment and watched the bubbles rush upwards in my drink. All day when I had tried to think of my work I had felt a kind of panic, and the more this gripped me the less able I had been to think straight. Instead of one idea opening into another, growing and developing, I had watched my thoughts close down, like some computer system into which a terrible virus had entered, blocking, deleting, destroying irrevocably. Now I felt no panic whatsoever.

I knew that the play would be about animals and their relations to humans, how we anthropomorphise them, how we project things onto them. I knew that this tended to happen more in the city than in the country, where people are less sentimental about animals. Our relationships with animals change the animals themselves. I thought about wild swans, about how they were truly wild, potentially angry and dangerous creatures, and how they never came looking for bread. I compared them with the swans one knew from the ponds and canals of cities, those sly, charming birds, constantly soliciting food.

And that was what had been so intriguing, I realised, about the man with the hare. I didn't know what the relationship between them was. Perhaps he had been going to kill it and eat it. Perhaps he had been going to breed it or to sell it. Or perhaps it was a pet, a companion, as a cat might be. Perhaps he was on his way to give it to someone as a gift, a bizarre love gift, like a woman in a fairytale asking for things she thought she could never receive, so as not to have to deal with the man's love. *Bring me gloves made of the skin of a fish. Bring me a wild hare that will follow at my heels like a lapdog.* Maybe he was going to kill it for its pelt. And the reason why I didn't know, couldn't even hazard a guess as to which of these was the real situation, was because the relationship between the two had been so neutral. The man did not tenderly stroke its fur, but nor did he appear to treat it harshly. It was impossible to know if the hare was still because of fear or trust.

And once, I remembered, when I was in France I had seen a sign for a lost dog with a full description and phone number. One line in heavy type said *Il est ma seule famille!* and for the rest of that day I hadn't been able to get it out of my mind. It upset me more than I would have thought it might, the idea of someone whose only family was a dog. And now that dog had disappeared. I gravitated back to the notice the following day and noticed another line that I hadn't seen on my first reading. *Attention! Il est très méchant avec les enfants!* So here we had a person whose only family was a dog which was extremely dangerous around children. Remembering this years later in Molly's back garden on a summer evening, drinking champagne with Andrew, I knew at once that this person would be the central character in the play I was going to write.

I instantly regretted that Andrew was there with me, that I couldn't simply go straight up to my desk and begin writing, now that I knew what I was about. Yes, the subject had suddenly fallen open before me, like a chestnut in its case that splits to reveal the clean white lining, the glossy brown of the nut, after days of trying to pick open tightly sealed prickly green cases. We were still sitting in silence. Andrew was staring not at me but at his drink, so I had at least time to think through all of this, and to try and fix it in my mind, in the hope of writing it all down as soon as he had gone.

'Molly says there's a hedgehog that lives in the garden,' I said. 'She told me it often comes out at dusk, but I haven't seen it yet.' Andrew raised his eyes from his champagne glass and looked at me oddly. I realised that while this remark was linked to the animal thoughts that were in my mind, it had nothing to do with anything I had said to him and must have struck him as bizarre.

'By the way,' I said, 'I bumped into an old friend of yours this afternoon. Marian Dunne.'

'Seriously?' I nodded, and he laughed. 'Did she ask after me?'

'She most certainly did. Wanted to talk about nothing and nobody else except you and your brilliant career.'

'You do surprise me. I wonder did she ever marry that medical student.'

I said that she had. I filled him in on the facts of her life, such as she had related them to me. It didn't take long. I told him she looked well but that she was bored with her life; that she had everything she'd set out to get – a husband, children, a big house, money, social position – and that it wasn't enough.

'Did she tell you this?'

'Don't be silly Andrew, of course not. But you didn't have to be a master psychologist to work it out.'

'Is she happy?'

'I wouldn't have thought so. No, not particularly.'

'Serves her right,' he said severely. I was surprised at this sudden flash of anger. 'It wasn't that she didn't want me because she didn't like me. I happen to know that she was very fond of me. I'm good enough for her now although I wasn't good enough for her then, but I'm still the same person.'

I made sympathetic noises, but I couldn't help thinking that there was such a thing as bad judgement. Andrew had always been a sucker for the kind of woman who has an ulterior motive, an agenda, and that he could never see this had always baffled and at times irritated me. I said as much to Molly once and she said, 'He can't see it because he's a man and they're women. Even if you explained it to him he probably wouldn't be able to see it.'

Suddenly he said, 'Look at the difference between Marian and you. You're happy to be my friend now, but you were also happy to be my friend when I was a scruffy student with nothing going for me, and I know that if my life were to fall apart tomorrow, for whatever reason, you'd be there for me. That's real friendship. It took me a long time to discover how rare that kind of integrity is.' I was surprised and deeply touched by this. *Friendship is far more tragic than love. It lasts longer.*

With that, a dark thought came to my mind. What if Molly had asked him the same question she had asked me? She was capable of it. What if he hadn't lied? *Yes, we did sleep together, but only once. It was a long time ago. We were both students, and it meant nothing. Don't tell her I told you, though, or she'll kill me.* And I would, too, I thought, looking at him, his head averted as he gazed off down the garden at the fake cow and the raspberry bushes, at the pink roses clustered on the wall. There was no way I could ever know the truth about this. Molly would never tell me, and I couldn't possibly ask Andrew.

'Marian Dunne,' he said softly, and he laughed. 'Strange, all of that is like a lifetime ago now. It seems more distant than when Billy died, although it was around the same time. I suppose it's because I haven't thought of Marian for years, and there's not a day goes by that I don't think of Billy.' I didn't know what to say to this surprising admission. I couldn't remember the last time he'd mentioned Billy, and even then it would only have been a passing reference. When he spoke again a few moments later I thought it was to change the subject completely, because he said, 'Do you ever think about the energy there can be in things? Jewellery, or a piece of silver or glass, for example. I think about it sometimes in the course of my work. There's the pure aesthetic of the thing, but sometimes you can't help being aware of something more, as if it still means what it meant to the person who used to own it.'

I told him that there were mediums who claimed to be able to describe a person in detail, their character and their destiny, simply by handling an object they had habitually used. I had thought that he would briskly dismiss this, and to my surprise he said slowly, thoughtfully, 'Well, I don't think I could ever believe in that, but I certainly understand where it's coming from. Nicole hated antique jewellery. I used to suggest it as a gift, and she wouldn't hear tell of it. It was nothing to do with the design, it was the thought of other people having owned it, of it being emotionally loaded, that she couldn't bear. And that's fair enough. I respect that.' I didn't know where all this was leading, and then he said 'Do you remember when I left Ireland, that last night before I went to Cambridge? I stayed with you, do you remember?'

He wasn't looking at me as he spoke, and I made a point of not catching his eye as I replied.

'Yes.'

'Something happened just before I left home, something I've never spoken about to anyone. We weren't a demonstrative family, and when my father became all emotional about me leaving and about Billy I didn't know what to say. It embarrassed me, and even annoyed me a bit. I just wanted it to stop so I could pick up my bags and go. And then he said, "Your mother and I want you to have this." We were sitting at the kitchen table at the time, drinking tea, and my father was smoking a cigarette. He put his hand in his pocket and took something out, set it there on the oilskin tablecloth in the middle of all the spilt sugar and the cake crumbs. It was a ring. A gold ring.' Andrew gave a little laugh that was full of sorrow. 'It was without a doubt one of the ugliest things I'd ever seen in all my life. A clunky, heavy-looking thing; it spelt out the word "son" across the knuckle, and the sides of it were textured like bark.'

'It was well-intentioned though, I suppose,' I said.

'But you don't understand. It wasn't a gift for me. It was Billy's ring. They'd given it to him for his eighteenth birthday. I recognised it the minute I saw it. Billy was mad about it, he wore it all the time. He was probably wearing it when he was shot, but fortunately I didn't think of that until much later. There was a lot about the ring that didn't register with me until much later. Anyway, there we were, my father and myself, sitting at the table with this thing between us. I said, "I won't be able to wear it," and he said, "I know that. We just want you to have it as a keepsake."' In explanation, Andrew held up his hands to me. They were large and broad. 'Billy was a skinny little fellow. I'd never have been able to get any ring of his past the first joint of my finger. Oh, I can't tell you how much I didn't want to have this ring, and yet I couldn't see a way out of it. It was so unexpected that apart from the obvious thing of it being too small I couldn't think of any other excuse, any other reason not to take it. So we sat there in silence for a few minutes longer and then I said, "Thanks, Da." I picked it up and put it in my pocket. And then as far I can remember – the next bit isn't clear in my mind – he got a bit upset and went out of the room. I don't think we said goodbye to each other formally. I suppose the taxi I'd booked arrived and I just left.

'In the train going south, I was very conscious of this thing he'd given me. It made me feel guilty. Illogical, but there you are. I made a conscious effort not to put my hand in the pocket where the ring was.' He gave a huge sigh. 'And then I got to Dublin and you were there and we had a great couple of days before I left for England. On the ferry I went up on deck, and it did cross my mind to get rid of it then, just throw it over the side into the wake of the ship, but even I wasn't that stupid. Even I knew that that wouldn't be the end of it. And I knew that it would be a cruel thing to do, not to Billy, because Billy was past cruelty, but to my father. So it stayed there still in the darkness of my pocket, and when I was settled in Cambridge I took it out. I tossed it into the back of a drawer without looking at it or thinking about it, the way you might put aside a handful of loose change when you come back from a foreign country: something that there's no real point in keeping but that you can't quite bring yourself to throw away either.

'And then, although you may not believe this, I forgot all about it. I didn't forget about Billy, although to be honest I didn't think a great deal about him either. I was focused on my new life, my studies; I was completely caught up in all of that. In those early years after he was killed I didn't brood on Billy's death the way I imagine most people in my circumstances would have done; as I know my parents certainly did.' He considered this for a few moments and then went on. 'I think what I'm saying is that I didn't properly mourn him at the time. I don't think I could understand what had happened to Billy. And yet there wasn't a day passed when there wasn't something that would bring him to mind. I might see someone in the street wearing a Manchester United shirt: that was the team he followed. Or I'd be in a café and I'd see someone putting heaps of sugar in their tea the way he used to. But most often it was nothing at all. I'd be in the library working or walking home at dusk or maybe at some party or in a pub, and suddenly he'd come into my mind. Just the idea of him. All of this life going on, people drinking and talking and laughing, and Billy not being a part of it. Not being here. Not being anywhere. I didn't feel sorrow about it, I didn't feel anything at all, not for ages. Looking back now, that seems strange. But that's the way it was.

'A couple of years after I moved to Cambridge I was burgled. In my heart I was disappointed when I discovered that they hadn't stolen Billy's ring. It was lying on the floor in amongst a heap of other things, because the whole room had been turned over, drawers emptied and their contents picked through. I suppose the thieves decided that to try to fence a cheap ring like that would be more trouble than it was worth. So when I tidied up, it went back in the drawer again.

'I got together with Nicole. I finished my PhD, we moved to London and got married. Obviously I told her about Billy and what had happened to him, but she had no real interest or curiosity about the subject so we never talked much about it subsequently. It remained a very private concern of my own. I began to think a lot about the idea of brothers. When I was around you, for example, you always talked a lot about your family, in particular about that brother of yours who's a priest.'

'Tom.'

'Yes. Tom. Part of the problem with Billy and me had been that we were so different. I'd always thought when he was alive that we had nothing in common and that that was why we had never got on. I could see that your life and Tom's were completely different and yet you were close. What was that like? I couldn't begin to imagine. And then something happened that began to change everything. Tony was born.'

He fell silent at that. He drained his champagne and moved to pour more into his own glass and then mine. I realised that he'd waited years to find the right person and the right time and place to talk about all of this. I was careful to say nothing that might disturb the tenor of the moment. I sat quietly until he was ready to continue.

'Although I had been looking forward to the baby being born, I had completely underestimated how I would feel towards him. I hadn't known that it would be so powerful. I hadn't realised that it was possible to love anyone with that degree of intensity, to care for them and for their well-being so much. But there was something about him that made all this even more peculiar. From the moment Tony was born, he looked like Billy. I can't tell you the shock that was to me. It never occurred to me that that might happen, I just hadn't thought about it. But he had Billy's ears and his nose; within a few days he was smiling at us with that same cheeky grin of Billy's. Here he was, a miniature version of the dead brother I'd never much cared for, and I'd have walked through fire for him.

'I began to think about that ring at the back of the drawer. Still I couldn't bear to look at it, but I thought about what it meant, above all I thought about that word "son". It began to dawn on me that I wasn't so special, that my parents had no doubt felt about Billy the way I felt about Tony. And then when I thought about what happened to Billy . . .' His voice trailed away; he couldn't bear to follow through and articulate the thought. After a moment he continued. 'One really good thing that came out of it all was that Tony brought about a kind of reconciliation between me and my parents. They were also overwhelmed by the family resemblance that was there. It endeared Tony greatly to them, but I could also see that they loved him for his own sake. They were both getting on in years by then and not in great health, so they weren't able to travel. I used to take Tony over to Belfast to visit them. That didn't go down too well with Nicole. She didn't much care for them, she thought they were vulgar and I didn't have much of a defence there, because I'd also thought the same thing for years. I didn't have too much time left with my family anyway. By the time Tony was three my mother had passed away, by the time he was five my father was also dead. My marriage was in serious trouble by then too, as you'll recall. Tony can't remember either of my parents, which is a pity, but I always remind him that they did spend time together. Just because you can't remember something doesn't mean that it never happened or it wasn't important. Those early years are crucial, and for Tony my parents had a part in them. And that means a lot to me.'

He fell silent again, and as he sat there quietly thinking about all of this, I almost did something extraordinary, something that might have ruined the delicacy of the moment. I almost closed my hand gently over his hand, where it lay resting on the table. I had actually done this once to someone many years before: an actor, a timid bore, with whom I was having a drink after a rehearsal. Molly had been there too. I hadn't been listening to what this man was saying; I was letting Molly carry the burden of the conversation. I'd been in love with Louis at the time. I was to meet him later that evening, and I'd been thinking about him while staring absently at the actor's hand on the table, thinking about him with tenderness and a great physical longing. And then some kind of weird disassociation took over. I forgot that the man's hand on the table before me didn't belong to the man I was thinking about. I reached over and softly closed my hand over his.

As soon as I touched him I awoke to what I had done. The shock of its not being my lover's hand went through me as unpleasantly as a bolt of electricity. I heard the man's voice falter, but he went on talking. I could sense his fright. Still I didn't draw my hand away. I looked at Molly. Her eyes had gone wide and round, like the eyes of some small exotic creature, a lemur or a meerkat. I could sense the hilarity under her astonishment. *Please don't laugh*, I pleaded with her, in my mind and with my gaze. *Whatever you do, please don't laugh*. I counted to ten and then I lifted my hand away slowly and carefully, like someone who has just finished building a house of cards. We all pretended that nothing untoward had happened. The actor said goodbye and left us a short while later. I don't think I've ever laughed so much in all my life as I did with Molly after he'd gone.

This time was different. This time I would have meant it. And this time I had the sense to keep my hands to myself.

'I hope you don't mind me talking about all this,' he said.

'No, not at all.'

'I may have given you the impression,' he said, 'that

after Tony was born I began to come to terms with what had happened to Billy, but that wasn't the case. Something else happened, years later, that brought it all to a head. Nicole and I had been living apart for about five years, so Tony would have been about ten by then. It happened in Paris. I had gone there for a month that summer, to do some research for the project that I was working on at the time; there were drawings there that I needed to see. I had taken a small apartment near the Observatory as a sub-let, but I didn't know the person who owned it. It belonged to a friend of a colleague of mine, and the rental was arranged through him: a fine apartment, in one of the old Haussmann buildings, with high ceilings and lovely plasterwork. There was stained glass in the stairwell and one of those marvellous old lifts with a metal gate. You could see each of the floors pass as you creaked your way up and down. I was at the top of the building, and there were chestnut trees just beyond all the windows.

'Not long after I got there, I realised that I didn't know anybody in Paris. That is, I had a few contacts through my work, formal professional contacts: a man I had met at a conference in Rome some years earlier, a woman who worked in the Louvre whom I had helped when she came to London. Perfectly pleasant, good colleagues, but not people I knew well. It didn't bother me in the slightest because I was extremely busy while I was there, and when I wasn't working I was never at a loss for things to do. I wasn't lonely. To be honest, it was a relief to be completely alone for a while, and there's no better city for it than Paris. You get treated decently, you can sit alone in a café for hours and no one will think anything of it. From time to time I would fall into conversation with people, locals or people like myself who were just passing through. No,' he said, as though I had contradicted him on this, although I had said nothing at all, 'I was happy during those weeks, and had it not been for what then happened, it would have remained in my memory as a good time.

'On the day in question,' he went on, 'I had wrapped up a particular piece of work around lunchtime and decided to take the rest of the day off. I had been in town just wandering about, reading in cafés, looking in bookshops. It was late afternoon, early evening when it happened. I was tired and beginning to think about going back to the apartment. I had salad at home, and a chicken; I would buy some bread and wine. I was passing a baker's and thought I'd get the bread there. I remember there was a café next door to the baker's, with tables and chairs outside on the terrace, and I stood for a moment looking in through the window at all the cakes.' For the first time since he started speaking he suddenly seemed hesitant and shy, as though what he was about to say embarrassed him. 'Just before it happened, I was thinking about you.' He laughed, but forced himself to follow through and say exactly what this meant. 'I almost died, and if I had, you would have been the person I was thinking of as it happened. There were some of those typical French *pâtisseries*, you know, open flans with strawberries piled up on them, lemon pies and the like. There were apple pastries, with slices of fruit overlapping like slates on a roof, and all glazed; and they reminded me of you because you like apples more than anyone else I know. I thought of how my earliest memories of you have to do with apples, of how, when we were at Trinity, you used to carry your stuff around in a green cord bag and you always had apples in it. You often used to skip meals. A cup of coffee and cigarettes and a few apples, and that would be your lunch, do you remember? After looking at the cakes I changed my mind, and decided I'd buy the bread nearer home. I turned away from the baker's window, took three steps past the café and then the bomb went off.

'It was out of sync – it blew me off my feet, and only then did I hear the sound of the explosion. As I went down I hit my head on either a chair or the edge of a table. Either way it knocked me out, but just for a split second, and it probably saved me from worse harm, because I fell at an angle on my shoulder, and as a result didn't hit my head on the pavement. I came to almost immediately, but I didn't know where I was nor what the hell had happened. I was lying on the pavement looking up at the sky, and I could see the legs of the café chairs and the metal feet of the round tables just inches from where I lay. Looking in the other direction, I was at the bottom of a big tree, with a great circle of decorative cast iron over its roots. It was this that reminded me that I was in Paris. It wasn't that I was comfortable there, far from it, but the energy required to get myself up off the ground seemed more than I was capable of at that moment. I wanted to stay there, but people were running past screaming, and someone almost kicked me in the head, so I hauled myself up and sat on one of the chairs. My trousers were torn but I felt OK, no pain, just sort of numb. My ears were really sore from the noise of the blast and I couldn't hear properly. I suppose I was in shock, though I didn't realise it at the time. As far as I was concerned I was just exhausted, like I hadn't had a night's sleep in a month and I wanted to stay sitting there. The emergency services seemed to kick in almost immediately. The place was swarming with policemen, there were ambulances, sirens, flashing lights all over the place. A helicopter came in to land near Notre-Dame, and I realised then how very near I'd been to the bomb itself.

'I'd obviously heard bombs when I was growing up in Belfast, and I'd been caught up in things, scares and riots and stuff, but this was the closest call I'd ever had. And even as I was sitting there the irony of that struck me. My whole life had been a kind of flight from the north and everything that happened there. I'd studied hard so that I could become what I knew I needed to be. Life had brought me at last after so many years here to Paris, to look at some drawings, and I'd almost been killed in a bomb blast as a result, in a dispute that had nothing to do with me. Then I thought about Billy and how he had died, even though for years I had actively tried not to think of him. I rarely felt sorry or sad about him, just angry and disgusted at the waste of a life. And suddenly I felt the whole loss of him in a way I'd perhaps never allowed myself to feel it before. It was just awful. I couldn't bear it. I stood up and walked away from the café, just to distract myself, just to be doing something.

'I was beginning to feel really stiff and sore, like I'd been beaten up. My head hurt. A lot of time seemed to have passed since the bomb exploded, but I realise now that it can only have been a matter of minutes. There were people around who were screaming and crying, but most were like me, silent and dazed, wandering around not knowing where they were going. There was a sense of calm that was more eerie and weird than the screaming. I saw a woman who was kneeling beside a man, cradling him in her arms, soothing him, and then I saw that all of his left arm, from the elbow down, had been blown off. I turned away and I saw another man who was also sitting on the ground. He said something to me urgently, and although I speak pretty good French I didn't understand what he was saying. He repeated it, and then he touched his temple with his fingers and pointed at me. I also touched my right temple, and then I realised what he had been trying to tell me, for when I looked at my hand it was drenched in blood. I must have cut my head when I hit the chair on the way down, and although my shirt and jacket were soaked I hadn't even noticed. My hand was dripping blood,' he said again. 'I looked as if I'd murdered someone.' He gave a rather dry ironic laugh. 'This will amuse you. When I saw the blood my first reaction, quite honestly, was that I had never before seen such a fabulous colour. I could be bleeding to death and all I can think about is how extraordinarily beautiful my blood is. It was like the colour of life itself; I couldn't get over it. The man who had pointed it out to me pulled a tablecloth off a café table and handed it to me. He was talking to me in French, and I remember I kept thanking him in Italian, but I didn't realise it until much later that night.

'So now what was I to do? With hindsight, remembering how confused and disoriented I was, I'm surprised at how clearly I was then able to think. I knew that the hospitals would be in a state of emergency, and that I didn't want to go there. I was wounded but not, I hoped, too badly. If I hung around I would be forced to get into an ambulance, so I decided to make myself scarce. The traffic was already completely snarled up, and I reckoned that the métro, at least in that part of town, would immediately have been closed down. As I say, I'm surprised at how clearly I was able to think and reason. I decided I would walk home. The man who had handed me the tablecloth tried to stop me walking away. I think he wanted me to go to the hospital, but that just strengthened my resolve. I pulled away from him and disappeared into the crowds.

'I don't know how long it took me to walk home, and I don't know how I did it. Out of the whole thing, that's the only part that's a bit hazy in my memory. People were staring at me. A man approached, he wanted to help me but I pushed him away and told him to leave me alone. I had only one thought now, to get back to the apartment. There was no one around when I got there, and I was glad of that, no one saw me enter the building. When I went into the actual apartment and saw myself in the hall mirror I got a shock, because I don't think I'd quite realised until then the state I was in. At least I'd stopped bleeding, it was dried and crusted on my face.

'My first thought then was to call Tony, but as I reached for the receiver the phone rang. It was Nicole, and I could hear someone sobbing in the background. "There's just been a news flash," she said. "It appears there's been a bomb attack in Paris. Because you're there, Tony's got it into his head that you've been killed."

"Let me speak to him," I said. Nicole went off the line, and I could overhear her saying to Tony, "Didn't I tell you that you were being stupid? Didn't I tell you there was nothing to worry about?"' Andrew took a deep breath. 'In spite of all we've been through, I still esteem Nicole and I respect her as Tony's mother. And so it pains me to have to say this, but sometimes she can be rather cold.' I nodded sympathetically but had the sense not to endorse this.

'The poor child, when he came to the phone he was crying so much he could hardly speak. I told him I was fine. I lied and said I'd been at home all day, just to reassure him. He kept saying, "I'm sorry, Daddy, I'm sorry," shame I suppose for crying, for being, as Nicole said, stupid. It was hard for me to hold back, but I was aware that if I let myself become upset and emotional he'd know I wasn't telling the truth about the bombing. "It wasn't silly of you to worry about me," I said. "It was loving and kind." To get off the line I told him there was something in the kitchen I needed to attend to, and promised to ring him again the following day.

'It was only when I came off the phone that I realised what a state I was in. Tony had managed to blurt out that he'd heard on the news people had died in the bombing. I'd feared as much, but it rattled me to have it confirmed. I suppose I did begin to realise that I'd had something of a narrow escape, and how incredible that would have been, to come from where I come from and to end up maimed or killed here. Then I looked in a mirror again and noticed that I was still a total mess.

'Never was I so glad for a few creature comforts. The person who lived in the apartment had left the bathroom pretty much as it was, with all kinds of toiletries and things, and I'd scrupulously not touched so much as a cotton wool bud. Now I just raided the cabinet. There was everything I needed, gauze, cotton, antiseptic, the lot. There was a box of some kind of salts, and I helped myself to that, ran a hot bath and poured it in. By that stage everything was really hurting.'

'How badly injured were you?' I asked.

'Not very. The cut looked worse than it actually was.

My shoulder was sore from where I'd fallen on it, and I had a terrible headache from having hit the edge of the table as I went down. It was as if I'd been beaten up in terms of both the physical pain and the sense of deep shock I felt. The bath didn't help as much as I'd hoped it would. Afterwards I poured myself a large whisky, which probably wasn't a great idea, but I was desperate for a drink. And then something quite strange happened.

'The apartment itself began to disturb me. As I've told you, up until then I'd been quite contented in it. That it belonged to strangers about whom I knew nothing hadn't troubled me in the slightest, but now it was precisely that which bothered me. Everything there was charged with the presence of these people whom I'd never met. There was a sofa upholstered in yellow silk that was slightly frayed at the armrests. There was a candle in a small pot of thick glass that had been lit at some point in the past and then extinguished. There was an intimacy about all these things, but one that I couldn't connect with because I didn't know the people who owned them, and that failure to connect was deeply unsettling. It made the whole apartment feel more anonymous to me than any hotel room could ever have been; and anonymity was the last thing I wanted that night. There was a peculiar stillness, too, a heightened quality, as though I were sitting in the middle of something distant and perfected. The room was beautiful and mysterious and still; but as for me, I was distraught, I was broken and grieving.' Even just remembering it and talking to me about it, Andrew was clearly upset. 'What followed was easily the worst night I've ever experienced in my life.

'I didn't go to bed. I was afraid of falling asleep in case

I had concussion, so I sat on the sofa all night until dawn. I desperately wanted to ring Tony, but that was out of the question. We're acutely sensitive to each other. Having managed to persuade him that everything was all right, I knew that if I spoke to him again, particularly in the frame of mind in which I now was, he would pick up on it immediately. I couldn't upset him just in an attempt to console myself. That wouldn't have been fair.'

'You should have called me,' I said.

'I did think of it. Then I remembered that you'd gone to Australia for a month. If it happened now I would call Molly. I thought about a couple of other friends, but in the end I rang no one. That was one of the things that made the night so lonely and painful. I realised how few people there were upon whom I could call when I was in trouble. All of this happened at a particularly low point in my life generally. I was still shell-shocked from the marriage having ended, and my career was in the doldrums. I was bored with the museum work, and the television thing didn't open up until the following year. Of course now that I'm successful,' he went on ironically, 'I suppose there's no end of people I could ring if I felt the need, and they'd be happy to help me. From what you say, I could even ring Marian Dunne. I couldn't have been lonelier or more upset that night if I'd been lost in a forest, rather than holed up in a comfortable bourgeois apartment in the middle of Paris.

'I felt so far from home. I started to think about Billy, I mean really think about him, not in that abstracted, almost wistful way he used to come into my mind, but Billy himself, just as he was. I wondered what he would have been like had he lived. Would we have got on any better? He might have settled a bit, got married, children, who knows? I was always so angry in those days when we were growing up together, pushing myself, desperate to get away, and I can see now why we didn't get on. Billy was the exact opposite of me: happy-go-lucky, always cracking jokes, a real live wire. He energised any company he was in. I started to mourn him that night. It was as if I'd been numb for all those years and only then begun to feel the pain of his loss. That he'd had such a violent death bore in on me. I remembered the ring my father had given me and I wished I had it with me. I think it might have given me some sort of comfort, some sort of connection amongst all those things in the apartment that meant nothing to me. I had the idea that when I got back to London I'd take it out of the drawer and from that day on, I'd keep it with me at all times.'

And now he took the ring from his pocket and set it on the table. It was just as he'd described it, a chunky, vulgar thing, solid and bright. I was glad he hadn't handed it to me because I didn't want to touch it. 'A lot of things came together that night. Billy's ring went from being something I didn't want to being something very precious to me. Billy's death became integrated into my life in a way that it should have been years earlier, only that I'd been too obtuse and resistant up until then. All the pieces were vaguely in place, but it took the shock of that night to pull them all together. Apart from this,' and he indicated the ring, 'what was there by which to remember Billy? A few faded photographs, and a headstone over the family grave, a place I never visited. I started to think about how people disappear, and then how they're forgotten or remembered; the things we make in their memory, the way we try to honour them. By the way,' he said suddenly, 'to this day Tony doesn't know about what happened in Paris, and I'd appreciate it if you didn't mention it to him.'

Unbeknownst to Andrew, I'd already made a similar promise to Tony to keep secret from his father a conversation we'd had about a year earlier. I've known Tony all his life, and he regards me as something of an honorary aunt. Molly knows him well too, but she would strongly resist such a concept in relation to herself. When they're together she flirts shamelessly with him, something he clearly finds embarrassing and thrilling in equal measure. Andrew and I were going out to lunch together on that day and had arranged to meet at his house. Tony opened the door to me when I arrived, and explained that his father had rung a short while before to say that he was running late. 'He'll be here as soon as he can.' Tony led me into the drawing room, formal with its gilded mirrors and dark furniture, a room that for me he had unconsciously humanised with his attendant clutter. There was an open bag on the floor with textbooks spilling out of its maw on to the rug. On a little table sat a mug of tea and a massive, half-eaten, crudely made sandwich, with bits of lettuce and ham hanging out of it. Tony politely ignored this until I urged him to continue with his lunch, and then he set to it with extreme and casual appetite. We chatted about his studies – he had exams coming up – and he told me that he was more interested in science than in arts and that it was something of a running joke between himself and Andrew. 'I don't know how much he means it, though. That is, I don't know if he'll be really disappointed if I don't follow him into the arts.' I said I felt sure Andrew would be happy with whatever choice he made, that he would rather Tony had his own interests and followed through on them rather than trying to please his father.

He swallowed the last of the sandwich, and then he said without any warning or preamble whatsoever, 'Did you ever meet my uncle?' This was so unexpected that for a moment I had no idea as to which uncle he might be referring: I thought that he might mean a brother of Nicole's. 'Which uncle would that be?'

'Uncle Billy.'

'Why no, Tony, I didn't. I never met your uncle.'

'But you know who I mean?'

'I do, of course.'

'You know he was murdered?' His face as he said this was strange, half grieved and half excited, and I didn't like the excitement.

'Yes,' I said shortly.

'You must remember the time when it happened, because you were at college with my dad.'

'You should ask Andrew about all of this, not me.'

'I don't want to upset him. If he felt all right about talking to me about it then he'd bring up the subject himself, wouldn't he? But he never does. It's important for me because it's my family too, you see.' I thought about this for a minute and then I said, 'I'll tell you what I know, Tony, but it isn't much.'

I described to him in some detail that Saturday evening so many years ago when I'd met Andrew on the street and gone with him to his house. I told him how cold it had been, how the sky had been deep pink as the sun set and how all this had happened just before his uncle was killed. I knew that what I was telling him was important, even though it was indirect, allusive, because it would help to put the bald fact of Billy's death into an imaginative context for him.

'Don't tell my dad,' he said again, 'but I went to the newspaper library and looked up that date. There wasn't much in the English papers but I was able to get to see some of the Irish papers on microfilm, and there was more there. It was so weird, seeing his name and thinking, "That's my dad's brother. That's my uncle."'

'All of this must seem quite unreal to you.'

'It doesn't. That's the problem. It seems completely real but I can't get at it, somehow.'

'They weren't particularly close, Andrew and Billy. They didn't get on.'

'I know that. I imagine that must have made it even more difficult for Dad.'

'Sometimes family things aren't easy.' He looked at me straight-faced, this child of divorced parents, this veteran of family life, and politely agreed with me. Andrew would have done anything for Tony. He lived in comfort, was sent to the best of schools; both his welfare and his pleasures were carefully considered and lavishly provided for. The one thing Andrew couldn't do for his son was to protect him from what he himself was, from the strange evolution and deep grief of his own life. Sometimes the most important and powerful element is an absence, a lack, a burnished space in your mind that glows and aches as you try to fill it.

'How much have you talked to your dad about this?'

'Hardly at all. I've always known about it. I mean, I sort of grew up knowing that my dad had had a brother, and I knew what had happened to him, but I didn't really think about it much. You don't understand these things when you're a little kid. Just recently I've been trying to get my head round it, but like I said, I don't want to upset him. Promise me you won't tell him we talked about this.'

'I'll do no such thing. I'll tell him he needs to tell you everything he knows about Billy.'

'No, please, promise.' There was the sound of Andrew's key in the door, and Tony stared at me in alarm. '*Please.*' I relented, and against my better judgement hissed 'Promise' as Andrew came into the room. He was completely preoccupied with being so late and didn't notice the atmosphere between Tony and me.

Because both our lives were so busy, although I had seen Andrew a few times since that day when I talked to Tony, this drink in Molly's garden, on her birthday, was the first private and considered meeting we had had since then. 'The next time you see Tony,' I said, 'tell him about Paris.'

'But I lied.'

'Explain why. He was a child. He'll understand now. He's not a child any more. You should talk to him about Billy, too. Show him the ring. Tell him the whole story behind it, just as you've told it to me. Tony has a right to know about these things. They're a part of his life too, his identity. He needs to know.'

'A couple of months ago he said he wanted to go to Belfast.'

'Did you take him there?'

'I ignored it. I thought he was pulling my leg. You know, I thought I was getting to the bottom of things, but it seems I'm still evading them. Billy was the whole idea behind the memorials series. All the time I was working on the project about portraits and then the landscapes, at the back of my mind there was always the thought of how people are memorialised, and all of that came from Billy. And yet when we made the series and I wrote the book, his was the one death that I couldn't bring myself to address. You see,' he said to me, 'there's something I don't think you're really considering here, and I very much doubt if Tony's aware of it either. Billy was killed. But it's also highly likely that he himself killed people too. He was deeply involved in Loyalist paramilitary activity, there's not the slightest doubt about that. Coming to terms with the idea that he was murdered was one thing. That he killed people, innocent people, is something else entirely. I still don't know how I'd explain that to Tony, how I'd help him cope with it. And that's why I avoid talking to him about his uncle.'

'It's great that the book is dedicated to him,' I said, and he laughed.

'I suppose so. What kind of expiation is that? The best I could manage, but it would have been meaningless to the Billy I remember. Maybe I did it for myself. That's one thing the making of this series convinced me about – that memorials of any kind have more to do with the living than with the dead.'

The heat had gone from the day, but warmer tones had come into the light, deep golden, as the evening wore on. Everything in the garden, the trees, the table, the fake cow, threw bizarrely long, distorted shadows. Near where we sat there was a honeysuckle, all frail cream and yellow spikes, all heaped and clustered against the wooden lattice. Its fragrance sweetened and intensified as the day ended into a deep rich perfume; and there were roses too in Molly's garden, roses and stock. When I was growing up in the country there was woodbine in the hedges, honeysuckle's wild little cousin, its stubby spikes yellow and pink, its perfume even stronger than honeysuckle. These things never leave you. I remembered that night more than twenty years ago just before Andrew went away, when we sat drinking cheap wine in the rough garden of a rented house.

'One other thing about that night in Paris,' he went on. 'At one stage in the evening I turned on the television and I saw news coverage of what had happened. It made me aware of exactly what I had been caught up in, how near a miss I had had. It frightened and upset me; I turned it off almost at once. Months later, when I was back in England, I happened to be watching television and suddenly there again was footage of that evening in Paris, the helicopters, people distressed and crying, the buildings of the city and the sky exactly as they had been. But the film was being used as part of a broader documentary about terrorism and there was a soundtrack over it, a voice-over and music. The music changed everything. It was a kind of soft jazz; for me it trivialised the images, and I was incensed. I did something I'd never done before; I rang the duty office of the channel that was broadcasting it. I spoke to a bored woman there. "What exactly is your problem, sir? That we're showing a news documentary and using music over it? That's actually quite common in the media now." I told her not to be sarcastic. When she heard that I had been there on the day, that I'd been caught up in it, she thought that was my beef, which it wasn't, not really. I hung up in the end, I could get no change out of her, and I sat there alone on the sofa, so angry. And then I thought, "This *is* just because I was involved on the day." The woman was right, I had seen any number of broadcasts like this in the past and they hadn't bothered me in the same way. All of this happened before I worked in television myself and I suppose, with hindsight, it was a good thing. It made me aware of the sensitivities of trying to present other people's realities in a way that I wouldn't otherwise have understood. After all I've said,' he went on, 'you may find this hard to believe, but I don't often think about that night in Paris. The knowledge that came out of it is with me every day, but the event itself has become distant and strange. I don't like thinking about it, and I'll probably never mention it to you again.

'But there is something I want to ask, if I may, something about you that has always puzzled me. I've always envied you your relationship to your family,' he said, 'your closeness to them and the support they give you. And yet I have to confess I don't think I've ever understood it.'

I knew exactly what he meant. Yes, I was close to my family. I went back to visit them whenever I could, and when they were able, some of them came to visit me. We spoke to each other frequently on the phone. I knew all their news, both serious and trivial things: the results of hospital tests, the results of minor football matches. Unlike many in my circle I think I have always understood the value of formulaic conversation and how it can make for real communication. Such exchanges can forge a link with someone when there is deep affection but no real common ground. Andrew, with his impatient intelligence, would never understand this. But I know Molly would agree with me. Her relationship with Fergus is built upon a similar visceral warmth, the childhood bond that has never been broken. Closeness of that particular type is perhaps only possible with people one has known all one's life, when the bonds have been made before something in one's soul has been closed down by consciousness, by knowledge; a kind of closeness that can coexist even with dislike. Perhaps this was something that Andrew could understand, perhaps this was why he was haunted by the thought of Billy, but I wasn't sure that I could explain it to him.

Instead I said, 'I remember when I was a teenager, one of my sisters was already married. She was in her early twenties and she was expecting her first baby. We were at home together alone and she was talking about it, how excited she was, how much she was looking forward to it; and then she said, "When this child is born, my life won't count for anything any more. Everything will be for him. The only meaning my life will have will be in relation to the baby." Don't get me wrong, this wasn't a complaint, for she said it with delight. Her attitude was shocking to me for it was as if life was some sort of terrible problem, a burden, and she had discovered a way to evade it, to pass it on to someone else and to let them suffer it. And even then, even though I was hardly more than a child myself, I knew that that wasn't right. I remember that you were arguing with Molly one time about religion and you said that one's first and perhaps only moral responsibility was to be fully human. If you did that, you said, everything else followed on. If you ask me, I suppose I'd say that the only thing you have to do with your life is to live it. And my sister's attitude appalled me because it was a repudiation of that, and yet she felt fully justified and vindicated in doing it.

'She had a son about a week later, whom I love dearly, as I love all my nieces and nephews. But I think you can see what I'm getting at. Close as I am, I feel that I don't belong. When I look at my family, their lives seem to me like a dream, a beautiful dream, full of warmth and companionship, but a dream for all that. While this was happening all around me, while I was growing up in it, Tom was simultaneously giving me books, making me question things, making me think. Tom in himself had been a challenge, drifting in and out of the house from time to time, the respect the rest of my family felt for his calling keeping him at a distance from them, although they would have denied this. I know he felt it, for he told me so. I think Tom and I saved each other from the worst of the loneliness that comes from being part of a family where you don't fit in. He helped me to find a life of my own that was right for me, a life that was a balance between his rather austere consciousness and their unthinking warmth.'

'You're very fortunate.'

'I suppose I am. Have you ever spoken to Molly about this? She has a theory that everyone gets pretty well what they want in life because they make a point of doing so, but the problem is that a great many people either don't know what it is that they want or they won't admit it.'

'Yes,' Andrew said, 'Molly did talk to me about this. It's something that's very important to her, the idea of owning your own life, standing over the choices you've made and honouring them, owning your mistakes as well as your successes.'

A change had come over his face at the mention of Molly's name, and it was a look I recognised. The three of us had met up in a London hotel on a dark afternoon the previous December when snow was forecast. Andrew and I arrived first and we ordered hot chocolate against the bitter cold of the day. We sat in an alcove near a big window, which afforded little light. The room was small and dim, low-lit by wall sconces, and there was a candle burning on the table. It was all chintz and gilt; and as the chocolate was served a gentle snow began to fall. I have never got over my childish delight in snow, and at its first falling I cannot help a feeling of excitement I know to be absurd. And then Molly arrived. She was dressed in brown, a colour that suits her well. She wore a brown wool coat with a velvet collar and a small felt hat that would have defeated a lesser woman, would have made her dowdy, but Molly did honour to it even as she pulled it off and tossed it aside. *Snow! Chocolate!* We called for an extra cup, and she started eating the almond biscuits that had been brought to us. She was like nothing so much as a bird that day, a wren, all restless energy. What did we talk about? I have no idea. I only know that Andrew and Molly did most of the talking. I fell silent. I watched my friends, and I saw for the first time Andrew look at Molly in that particular way, that softness that he manifested today even when he was only thinking about her. How to describe it? Adoration, I suppose. Yes, adoration.

By now I was regretting the champagne. I felt fuddled, but not pleasantly so. I think I had hoped for – no, I think I had confidently expected – the cheerful euphoria the red wine had given us all those years ago, instead of which it had brought only a flat melancholy. Billy's ring was still sitting on the table. It was beginning to upset me, looking at it there. I couldn't help thinking of it as a thing full of bad energy. 'Don't forget that,' I said in the hope that Andrew would put it in his pocket immediately, and to my relief he did, but he also took it as a cue to leave which I certainly hadn't intended. 'I should make a move.'

'Stay here for a few minutes more,' I pleaded. We sat there in silence listening to the night around us, until the listening became active, meditative, an experience in itself. A dog was barking in the distance. A car passed on the road beyond the house. In a garden further down the street a group of people were also making the most of the longest day; we could hear their laughter, their voices. That short period of listening redeemed the evening for me. White flowers glowed in the low light: lilies, lobelia, stock's fragrant little stars. It all became peaceful and profound, and when the time was right it was I who suggested that we move into the house.

It was only when I stood up that I realised I'd had more to drink than I'd intended, even though I'd made sure that the lion's share of the bottle had gone into Andrew's glass. He moved to lift the tray, but I told him to leave it, and said that I would deal with it later. 'Come up to the drawing room for a moment,' I added. 'There's something I want to show you.'

The ceiling light would have been too glaring and harsh, so I switched on a small lamp sitting on a table beside a stack of books. The lamp was a fake antique, with a shiny metal base and a spherical globe of frosted glass, etched with swags of ribbons and flowers, the sort of thing I knew Andrew abhorred. I sat down in a low armchair beside the table, while Andrew wandered around the dim room inspecting everything. All the books were pushed well back into the bookcases and here and there, against the spines, Molly had propped postcards she had received: Sydney Opera House, Venice, a reproduction of a Cézanne still life. There were a few small photographs in amongst the postcards, mostly unframed snapshots of Molly herself, casual photos unrelated to her work, taken with Fergus or with friends. There was also a framed photograph of her father. Such invitations as she had recently received, including one to a garden party in London on this very day, she had placed in traditional manner on the mantelpiece. Andrew was gazing at a vase full of twiggy branches. He crossed to the window and picked up from the sill a lump of white quartz that Molly had found somewhere and that had taken her fancy. 'This is such a marvellous room,' he said, even though there was so much in it that he couldn't possibly like. Anyone could see, even someone who really didn't want to understand, what all this was about. These objects had value and beauty for him simply because they belonged to her, to Molly Fox.

'There was something,' he said, 'you wanted to show me.' There wasn't. I had only said that as a pretext for keeping him here for a little while longer. I heaved myself out of the chair and went over to the glass-fronted bookcase where Molly kept her most precious books, unlocked it with the small key and removed *The Duchess of Malfi*. 'Come over here to the light,' I said, 'and look at this.' I handed the book to him and he turned it over in his hands in that appraising professional manner he has when examining things. He stood there with his head bent and his eyes lowered, gazing at the book; and it afforded me an opportunity to look closely at him. I remembered how I used to watch him studying in the library all those years ago, when I'd been awed by his ability to concentrate. With hindsight it surprised Andrew too, for he'd said to me once that there was a type of intellectual single-mindedness of which one was capable only in one's early twenties and which was astonishing in retrospect. 'Although of course it's possible,' he went on, 'that it isn't an age thing, it's rather that having done it once you can never again motivate yourself nor find the energy to repeat it.' Not that I would know about that. His face in youth had been quite shut, stern even, as he frowned over his textbooks, closed off in his own mind from everyone around him. Since then the student's fair hair had faded and thinned. Physically he had never fitted the stereotype of the aesthete; he was too solidly built and powerful. His forehead was large and square. Those hands that held the book would never wear Billy's ring. I was suddenly aware of how his look had softened over the years, and why. All the tribulations he had been through, and they were considerable – his difficult relationship with his family, Billy's death, the failure of his marriage – had not embittered him. Andrew had won through to some kind of moral knowledge, and it had matured him. He had successfully integrated these shocks and disappointments not just into his life but into his self, his sense of who he was. It was quite an achievement. With that, he raised his head and looked at me.

'You've had a hard time,' I said.

'What do you mean?'

'Oh, everything that's happened,' I explained lamely, and he shrugged.

'It's only life.' He closed the book and handed it back to me. 'Molly has impeccable taste. And now I really must be on my way.'

We went out into the hallway, and he wished me luck with my play. Already the ideas I had had for it while I was sitting in the garden had lost their appeal: I was no longer sure that they would help me find my way into the work.

'I'll call you when we're both back in London. If you're talking to Molly, give her my love. Tell her I said Happy Birthday.'

He bent down and kissed me goodbye, a formal, polite kiss; and as he did so I remembered again that night I'd slept with him. Only this time it wasn't just the fact of it that came back to me. This time my whole body remembered, in a rush, a shock. It was like stepping onto something that wouldn't hold and falling through, and in that fraction of a second between his lips brushing my cheek and the front door closing behind him I caught his eye, and I couldn't be sure that he wasn't also remembering the same thing in the same way. Then he was gone.

There was a chair in the hall where no one ever sat, but I sat on it now; and the clock at the head of the stairs began to chime softly, first its warning chords, and then it struck ten times. I sat there in the absolute silence that fell afterwards, still in another reality, aroused and emotionally shattered. And that's how and where I was when the doorbell rang.

Andrew. He had come back.

I'd been correct, then, in what I'd sensed he was thinking as he left the house. But should I open the door to him? Was this what I really wanted? Who was I trying to fool? This was what I'd wanted for years. What had held me back until now was exactly this, waiting for some kind of cue from Andrew, and it had never been there until tonight. But would I really be able to go through with it? In Molly's house, of all places? In Molly's bed? It couldn't be helped, and in any case, she would never find out. The doorbell rang again and I realised with a start that he might think I was refusing him, he might go away again. I jumped up from the chair and opened the front door.

Standing on the front step was a woman, a complete stranger.

'Oh,' she said. 'I was looking for Molly Fox.'

'Well she's not here.'

'Oh,' she said again, and this time her disappointment was considerable, but still nothing like mine. There are no words that can do justice to the weird combination of grief and mortification that I was undergoing. I was also fed up with opening the door to people who were crest-fallen to find me on the other side of it, and then the woman said, 'But she does live here, doesn't she? This is her house?' and I saw that my annoyance was unreason-able. 'Yes,' I said, 'Molly Fox lives here.' Because I was at something of a loss to know what to do, I asked the woman to come in.

She stepped blinking into the light of the hall, and I realised that she was much older than I had at first thought. I had taken her to be in her mid-fifties, but she was at least ten years older than that. She was wearing a floral print cotton dress with a pale blue cardigan over it. 'I'm sorry to barge in like this, I know it's so late . . .' I brushed aside her apologies and brought her into the front room where the table lamp was still lit. The woman was carrying a light, shallow crate of the kind in which vegetables are sold, and it was full of little plants. As I gestured to her to sit down in the low chair that I had earlier occupied, she handed the box to me. 'I wanted to give these to Miss Fox. They're herbs – coriander, dill, mint, thyme and rosemary. I was going to bring her parsley but she's probably already got some, and I was going to bring her some basil but it had bolted.' The plants were damp, and she touched them as she spoke of them, releasing their fragrance, bringing into the house the fresh, earthy odour of the garden, of the warm summer night. Her broad hands were mottled with age spots, reminding me of the hands of my grandmother, my grandmother who had come to me in a dream that morning, also bearing gifts. I realised now that the woman was nervous and shy, that I had been somewhat brusque with her for no reason except for the ridiculous fact that she wasn't Andrew. I thanked her warmly for the plants as I took them from her, as she finally sat down. 'There's a punnet of strawberries, too, from my own garden, and a surfinia, a dark red one.'

'Molly will be delighted. She loves gardening.'

'I know. I sometimes see her out working at the front. That's how I knew that this was her house. I live near here and one day I was passing when I saw her out weeding. I've seen her in her garden a couple of times since then, and every time I walk down this road I think of her. When I pass this house I always say to myself, *Molly Fox lives here*.'

I noticed that she was paying no heed to the room.

Unlike Andrew, whose eyes had flickered around restlessly, looking at Molly's possessions, her mirror, her Chinese vases and her kilims, as if to know them was to truly know her, this woman seemed to register nothing around her. When speaking, she either looked straight at me or down at her own hands. I was sitting across from her, in a pocket of darkness beside the bookcase. I switched on a lamp that stood nearby, but I tilted the shade away from me. I realised that there was a chance, albeit slight, that the woman might recognise me, and I didn't want that. *I called to Molly Fox's house but she wasn't there. I met that writer, I can't remember her name, the playwright, you know who I mean, they've worked a lot together. She was in a strange humour; I think she'd been drinking.*

'I met her once,' she went on, and then she laughed in a self-deprecating way. 'That is, we spoke to each other. You could hardly call it a meeting. She'd been putting in bedding plants, violas, they were, purple with a little yellow star in the heart of each one. Just as I passed the gate she straightened up, she caught my eye. I said to her, "All you need now is a little shower of rain," and she laughed, looked up at the sky and said, "I think I'll get it before the day's out." We smiled at each other and I walked on. Such a voice she has! It was extraordinary to hear it, you know, just like that, not in the theatre or on the radio, but in the street, saying something very ordinary about the garden. Afterwards I was sorry that I hadn't said more. It was a chance for me to thank her, to tell her how much it's meant to me, seeing her on stage over the years. But I was only sorry in a way. I don't really know what people like her think about people like me.'

'I'm afraid you've lost me,' I said, and she smiled ironically.

'I'm a fan.'

It was hard to know how to reply to this. I shrugged and said, 'Most everyone likes to be told that they're good; they like to be praised and flattered.'

The woman looked down at her hands. 'Oh, I always think of what Auden said, you know? It's you they want to meet but themselves they want to talk about. I shouldn't like to come across in that way.'

'You don't.' I meant it too: this woman was out of the common run of fans.

She looked up at me again. 'I was so pleased after that little exchange the day she was planting the violas. You're the first person I've ever told about it, and I can't think she ever mentioned it to anyone else, because it was so slight, so inconsequential that there was nothing to tell, certainly on her side. I did once mention to my husband that I'd seen Molly Fox in her garden, but I didn't tell him we'd ever spoken to each other. I like to think that out of our whole lives, hers and mine, there was this little moment that only the two of us shared. If I'd mentioned anything about her acting it would have changed it and spoiled it. This is silly, I know. These things mean nothing. I always go to see any play she's appearing in here in Dublin; sometimes I go two and even three times. I have a son who lives in London, and when I visit him I always make a point of trying to catch one of her plays. Sometimes I plan a trip to coincide with a particular run.'

'Are your family also interested in theatre?' I asked.

'No, not at all,' she said. 'Play-acting, that's what my husband calls it. He doesn't like it that I go to the theatre.

He doesn't understand it, and he tries to make out I think I'm somehow better than him, which is absolute nonsense, of course.'

'Did you see *The Duchess of Malfi*?' I asked. I didn't feel comfortable with the direction the conversation had taken and I wanted to change the subject.

When she replied I thought she hadn't heard me, that she was still talking about her family, because she said, 'So much of life amounts to nothing, doesn't it? I mean really,' and she gave a little laugh, 'absolutely nothing whatsoever. You're locked into this iron routine, cooking and shopping and cleaning, saying things to people and them saying things back to you, and none of it meaning anything, all of it pointless. Maybe it has to do with getting older, I don't know. I feel like I'm sleepwalking through the years, but I want to wake up. Reality, you know? Why is it so hard to find? And why do so many other people not seem to notice this? Why don't they care? Yes, I did go to see *The Duchess*, and all of this was very much on my mind that particular evening. I was worn down with it all, I felt stultified. And then the play – well, Molly Fox in particular, she was electrifying. All that dullness, that unreality I'm talking about, she blew a hole through it with language, with that voice of hers; it was like an explosion going off in your soul. And to tell you the truth, I can't think why and I can't explain it, because the play itself is strange. It has nothing whatsoever to do with my life, the world I live in, and yet it touched me like nothing I'd ever experienced before.'

As the woman spoke I myself remembered being in the theatre the night I saw the play. The brassy music, cold, all horns and cymbals; the fires blazing in cressets, the black and red costumes, cloth of gold. I too had been struck by what the woman referred to: how something so artificial could also be so moving and true. On the evening I saw *The Duchess* I'd seen Molly briefly in her dressing room a short while before the curtain went up. She was already in costume and fully made-up. Seen close to and without stage lighting she looked peculiar, almost grotesque, with her eyes heavily painted and two hectic spots of rouge on her cheeks. She wore a heavy dress made from what looked like upholstery fabric for a pretentious hotel, with all the fake luxury of cheap red brocade and gold trims. Molly seemed diminished in the middle of all this, muted, as she always is just before she goes on stage. I had gone to her dressing room at her invitation, but our talk was inconsequential. She would ask me questions and then I would be aware that she was not listening to the answers. From time to time she would self-consciously reach up and touch the elaborate wig she was wearing. I left her with a little time to spare before she was due on stage. I understood why she had needed my company and, not for the first time, I wondered at the psychological toll acting was taking on her. She had confided in me once that if ever anything brought her career to a standstill it wouldn't be stage-fright, but the terrifying loneliness she would suffer sometimes just before she went on stage. This surprised me, given how solitary a person she is in her life, but she insisted that this was different, that it was a dark, malevolent thing that made her understand what Fergus went through in his depressions. She said that it was as if, in preparing to become someone else, she sometimes fell between two psychic states; or as if, to fully inhabit the personality of the character, she had to become alienated from her self. I told her I couldn't imagine what that must feel like. 'You don't want to know, believe me,' had been her short reply.

Later that evening, the alchemy of the theatre transformed the odd little creature I'd met in the dressing room into royalty. I agreed with the woman who had called to Molly's house tonight, never had I seen a finer performance. The seating of the auditorium was arranged in curved rows, and from where I was placed I was able to observe not only the stage but also the audience. I could see all the people by the light of the stage, their rapt faces, the quality of the attention they were giving to what they were watching. Each of them was making their own private connection with the work, each bringing their own experiences and emotions to bear upon the play, to interpret it and integrate it into their own imaginative life. That this was happening in the presence of so many other people was crucial. In the apprehension of art there can be a loneliness, as there so often is in its creation. This breaching of loneliness may be the secret of what an audience is, or at least one of its secrets. That night in the theatre when Molly appeared as the Duchess, I looked at the audience and I thought, nothing surpasses this.

The cry late in the play, *I am Duchess of Malfi still*, is another of those apparently simple but endlessly complex lines which are such a challenge for an actor. I wonder if there was anyone in the theatre who didn't have gooseflesh when they heard Molly say it. She gave it its full weight and significance, while still honouring its simplicity. There was defiance, an almost arrogant assertion of who she was, and astonishment too that after the loss of so much in her life, she had not lost her self. That woman up there, pretending, to put it crudely, to be a medieval duchess, was my friend, and I believed in her; believed in her as a duchess, that is. Her plight moved me, and yet still I knew she was an actor, someone whose home I visited and who talked to me about her garden, who never forgot my birthday and never wanted me to remember hers. *Who is it can tell me who I am?* Who was Molly Fox? That night she was communicating something of her deepest self in a way that is only possible for her when she is on stage. Is the self really such a fluid thing, something we invent as we go along, almost as a social reflex? Perhaps it is instead the truest thing about us, and it is the revelation of it that is the problem; that so much social interchange is inherently false, and real communication can only be achieved in ways that seem strange and artificial.

'I wanted to thank her,' the woman said, 'but I didn't want to intrude. I felt very shy about approaching her too, so I kept putting it off and making excuses to myself. Then this morning I saw her birthday listed in the paper. I knew she was here – well, I thought she was here because I passed the house a couple of nights ago and I saw an upstairs light on. I wanted to bring her a present, but what could I give her? I couldn't think of anything that someone like me could offer to Molly Fox.' She lifted her hand in a gesture that took in all the books and rugs and pictures in the room. 'I know she likes gardening, and so I thought then I'd bring her some herbs and plants. In the bottom of the box there's another thing too, a little token that I hope will please her. I got everything ready mid-morning, but I made the mistake of telling my husband. All day I kept putting it off. I said to myself that I'd go round to her house before the hour was out, and then the time would pass and I'd set myself another deadline and I'd let that pass too. And then about half an hour ago my husband said to me, "I knew you wouldn't do it. I knew you wouldn't go. You're always saying you'll do things and then you put them off. You never follow through." That annoyed me so much and I said to myself, "I'm going to prove him wrong. I *will* go, and I'll do it right this minute." I put on my cardigan and I came straight round. The only thing was,' she said, suddenly crestfallen, 'Molly Fox wasn't here.'

'I'll tell her you called, and I know that she'll be delighted with the plants.'

'It's probably just as well I missed her, because it might have been difficult. It's been better to talk to you.' I made no comment on this, for I couldn't think of a polite way to say that it was true. Molly is ill at ease with the public; and while she likes to receive letters and cards, and is punctilious about replying to them, her shyness undermines her when she meets people face to face. *Curiously unimpressive in herself, isn't she?* I once overheard a woman remark at a reception. It angered me because it wasn't fair. Molly is remarkably impressive in herself, but she doesn't make that self available to all comers. Sometimes she questions her own popularity. 'Why should people like me just because I can act? It makes no sense.'

'They like you,' I told her, 'because you give them something and they're grateful to have it. It's gratitude a lot of the time, rather than affection, and they may not even realise it themselves.'

'I really must be going,' the woman said, and she stood up. I saw her out to the front door with promises that I would look after the plants and communicate her good wishes to Molly. In the hall she noticed all the pictures and trophies, Molly's little museum to her own success. I believe she'd overlooked them when she arrived, possibly through nerves, but she stood for a moment now and briefly studied them, all the photographs and posters and pieces of bronze and cut glass. She was silent and clearly awed. When she left she more or less bolted from the house. I was still speaking to her, and it was only after she had gone that I realised I didn't even know her name.

I went back to the drawing room and collected the box of herbs, carried it down to the kitchen. As I lifted out each of the plants in turn and set them on the draining board, I remembered that the woman had said she had also brought along something else, and as I removed the last little pot, I saw with dismay what it was.

A feather. A peacock's feather, of all things. There it lay, with its air of evil glamour, its glossy black eye and jewel colours, as though precious stones, sapphires and emeralds, had been transformed by some dark art into this weightless veil of mobile light. Suddenly the visiting stranger appeared to me in a wholly different aspect, as malevolent, as the bearer of a bad omen. How could she have done such a thing? Didn't she know? Molly must never find out about this. She has a pathological fear around this particular superstition; it would upset her terribly. I had to get it out of the house, get rid of it immediately.

I picked it up. It was unimaginably light, like everything connected with birds, like birds themselves, and it waved and quivered in my hand as I carried it out into the back garden. To put it in the bin didn't seem definitive enough. It would still be on the premises, and a part of me did scruple to put a thing of such dark beauty in with all the rubbish, with tin cans and tea leaves. I picked my way down the garden as my eyes grew accustomed to the low light, until I came to a bench about halfway down, beside the fruit bushes. The bench was hard up against the wall that separated Molly's garden from the property next door. Moving quietly so as not to be heard, I climbed up onto the bench, from where I could just about reach over. I stretched my arm as far as I could, trying to hold my hand clear of the climbing plants that were growing up against the other side of the wall, and when I knew I could stretch no more, I released the feather. I hope it fell to the ground. I hope it didn't become tangled in ivies and clematis, giving the game away about how it had come to be there. As I climbed down from the bench and stole back up the garden, it struck me that what I had just done was rather mean-spirited. My only consolation was to remember that this was a particularly theatrical superstition and was perhaps not commonly known amongst the general run of people. Molly's neighbours might well be both delighted and mystified to find a peacock's feather lying in their back garden on the morning after the longest day of the year. I hoped that that would be the case.

When I went back into the house, I remembered that this was the night I was supposed to wind the long-case clock. I went up to the return of the stairs and took the key from the hook on the door jamb where Molly kept it. I opened both the glass disc over the dial and the long narrow door in the body of the clock, behind which the weights were concealed. Before I started to wind it, I studied the clock for a moment. Molly had once said that it was the one thing she would want to save if the house was on fire, which greatly amused Fergus. 'I have an image of you, Molly, going down the road in your nightdress, carrying a grandfather clock in your arms.' The face of the clock was the colour of parchment, and the metal hands were delicately wrought. Above the dial was a semicircular recess with a painted moon and a shooting star. The moon had a long, straight nose and rosy cheeks; it stared at me innocently. The two weights were fully extended on their cords. As I started to wind the clock first one ascended slowly and then the other. I thought of the day that was ending and how, as I rose, as I tried to work, as I walked the hot streets of the city and talked to Fergus, to Andrew, to the late-night caller, all that time these weights had been slowly descending. I thought of them being raised up and slowly falling all the days of our lives in other houses, other rooms: on the night Billy was shot, on the night I spent with Andrew, on the day Molly's mother left home, until it seemed to me that this dark, narrow wooden compartment held time itself.

Now I could hear the phone ringing, down in the hall. Could it perhaps be Andrew?

'I'm not disturbing you, am I? You weren't asleep?' said a familiar, extraordinary voice. 'I'm not exactly sure what time it is in Ireland now but I wasn't able to ring earlier.' I reassured Molly; I told her that a visitor had left only a short time earlier. 'Who was that?' she asked. I explained, and Molly seemed more interested than I would have expected; she was particularly touched by the gifts. She told me to eat the strawberries, which made me feel slightly – only slightly – less guilty about having drunk her champagne, and suggested a spot in the garden where I might think to plant the surfinia.

'What colour is it?'

'Dark red.' She was delighted at this; she had looked everywhere earlier in the year for just such a flower.

She told me that she had spoken to Fergus shortly before she rang me and that he'd told her he had seen me. 'He always finds this a particularly difficult day. I'm sorry I wasn't able to be there for him. I had told him you would be staying in the house; he must have forgotten.' I told her that Andrew had also called. 'What did he want?'

'He brought you a copy of his new book, the book of the series. Oh, and he brought you a bottle of champagne as well.'

'I hope you drank it,' she said. I laughed to hide my embarrassment, and Molly laughed too. 'Poor Andrew,' she said, and she said it in such a way that I knew she knew how much he idolised her; and I knew too that he hadn't a hope. 'He sends his love. He said Happy Birthday.'

'Did he, indeed?' Her tone was wary now. 'How did he know that today was my birthday? Did you tell him?'

'It was in the paper.'

'What! How old did they say I was?'

'Forty.'

She swore when I said this, a sudden, crude outburst. It was all the more shocking because Molly almost never swears. There was the incongruity of hearing such a thing uttered in that particular voice, and I realised that she was as capable of drawing forth all the ugly power an oath might contain as she could the beauty and tenderness of other words. 'I never heard such nonsense in my life. I'm only thirty-eight.' I wondered if this were true. I was gradually coming to realise that there was much I didn't know about Molly Fox, far more than I had imagined.

'How's New York?' I asked. 'Oh it's all right, I don't really know what I'm doing here, to be honest. I'm looking forward to getting to London and *Adam Bede*. I'm only ever really happy when I'm working. How about you, how's the writing?' I told her that I was struggling with it, that I had thought earlier in the evening that I had finally worked out a new idea for the play but that now I wasn't so sure. 'Maybe I'll do something completely different, something I've never done before. Maybe I'll write a novel.'

We wrapped up our conversation, and I thanked her again for loaning me her place. I told her about the broken jug, but she was dismissive about it. Afterwards, I walked through the house to the kitchen, where the wooden box, the fruit and plants, were still sitting on the draining board. There was a smell of earth and herbs. I crushed a spine of rosemary between my fingers and inhaled the fragrance, sharp, deep, with something of the heat of the south in it; and I smiled to myself to remember Andrew doing the same thing, so cautiously, earlier that evening. Absentmindedly I picked up one of the strawberries and bit into it, into the red flesh with its scented white core, and then I wandered out into the garden. There was still light in the sky, a pure blue radiance. I sat down and ate the second half of the strawberry. The cow looked even more peculiar than it did in broad daylight. The two empty glasses were still there on the table, and the neck of the champagne bottle stuck at an angle from the chrome bucket. All the ice had melted back into water.

And then I heard something rustle nearby at the bottom of a trellis. Lumbering, slightly awkward but moving with surprising speed nonetheless, it was a hedgehog. It had noticed me now, and it came to a complete standstill. Even when I stood up and moved towards it, it didn't budge, and so I was able to inspect it at my leisure. How strange it was, with its crown of brown spines and its bright eyes, its squat feet and pointed snout. It looked completely *other*, like a creature that had arrived not from a burrow beneath the ground, but from another planet. I moved closer again and still it stood there, immobile. It was only when I drew back that it scampered off once more. At the foot of a climbing rose it came across the champagne cork that had shot off into the undergrowth when Andrew opened the bottle. The hedgehog stopped for a moment, sniffed it, tapped it with its foot, sniffed it again. Inscrutable, mysterious, it moved on once more and then disappeared into the shadows and was gone.

ff

Faber and Faber – a home for writers

Faber and Faber is one of the great independent publishing houses in London. We were established in 1929 by Geoffrey Faber and our first editor was T. S. Eliot. We are proud to publish prize-winning fiction and non-fiction, as well as an unrivalled list of modern poets and playwrights. Among our list of writers we have five Booker Prize winners and eleven Nobel Laureates, and we continue to seek out the most exciting and innovative writers at work today.

www.faber.co.uk – a home for readers

The Faber website is a place where you will find all the latest news on our writers and events. You can listen to podcasts, preview new books, read specially commissioned articles and access reading guides, as well as entering competitions and enjoying a whole range of offers and exclusives. You can also browse the list of Faber Finds, an exciting new project where reader recommendations are helping to bring a wealth of lost classics back into print using the latest on-demand technology.